THE FAIRMONT MANEUVER

SCOTT STILETTO 2

BRIAN DRAKE

D1737137

WOLFPACK
PUBLISHING
— EST 2013 —

The Fairmont Maneuver
(Scott Stiletto 2)
Brian Drake

Wolfpack Publishing
6032 Wheat Penny Avenue
Las Vegas, NV 89122

Paperback Edition

Ebook ISBN: 978-1-64119-627-7
Paperback ISBN: 978-1-64119-628-4

THE FAIRMONT MANEUVER

Switzerland – The Beginning

LARS BLASER KNEW that the dark-haired woman with the long legs worked at the US Embassy in Bern. He didn't know that the CIA paid her salary. That would be a bonus, the benefit of which he would soon discover.

Lars followed her from the embassy to Adriano's Bar & Café on a sunny Thursday. He noticed nothing of the pleasant day around him. All he wanted was to talk to somebody who worked at the embassy, but he couldn't just show up at the door because the Iranians were watching. If he met her away from the embassy, maybe they would think he was having an affair with her.

He laughed at the thought. He was a university physics professor, not the kind of man who had affairs with pretty brunettes with long legs.

The woman sat outside, her back to the café's white stucco outer wall, reading an English language magazine. A waiter buzzed in and out of the arched entrance, serving the outside tables. The woman had placed her purse on the table with the opening close to her right hand. Nothing made her stand out from the other patrons, except maybe her business suit, which seemed out of place with the surrounding tourists in street clothes. Her long hair was tied back, strands falling alongside her face, and she had brown eyes and a small nose. She scanned her surroundings every few minutes.

The tourists, busy with maps and menus written in German as well as their food, which they attacked with gusto, didn't notice him as he approached. He stepped through the gap in the knee-high divider that bordered the sidewalk.

He wasn't entirely nondescript. Tall, middle-aged, and a little paunchy, he wore a light tweed jacket, tan slacks, and a white shirt. He'd forgotten to remove the yellow university security badge from his jacket lapel, which displayed the University of Bern's logo, a lower-case U with a raised B above, his name in smaller type below.

He hesitated for a moment as he neared the woman's table, but he had no other ideas. He needed help badly.

The legs of the extra chair scraped loudly on the concrete as he pulled it back. As he sat, she gave him a startled look and reached for her purse.

What he said stopped her hand.

"The Iranians want me to build them a bomb," he told her. "You have to help me."

The words took a moment to sink in. She blinked a few times, then said, "I'm sorry, what?" She leaned closer, magazine forgotten, but her hand remained close to the purse.

Blaser's voice shook as he went through his memorized speech. "My name is Lars Blaser. I'm a physicist at the university. My life is in danger. Two days ago, an Iranian named Shahram Hamin said he would kill my family and me if I did not help his country make a nuclear bomb."

"That's very interesting," she remarked.

"You work at the US Embassy. I followed you here. Tell the Americans. I need help. I can't do it."

"Can't, or won't?"

"Won't. I can build a bomb blindfolded, that's not the problem. But what they want—"

The woman completed the reach into her purse and brought out a pen and a crumpled envelope. She straightened the envelope and handed him both items.

"Name and telephone, and somewhere else we can reach you."

"You promise?"

"You picked the right person to follow, Mr. Blaser."

Blaser provided his information, and then the woman told him to leave. He rose stiffly but with relief on his face and walked away.

THE WAITER BROUGHT HER ORDER, the Lord Sandwich with roast beef and tartar sauce, and Jennifer Turkel asked for a takeaway box. Emergency at work and all that. The waiter suppressed an annoyed frown but complied.

On the walk back, she called her boss to explain the surprise meeting, and he told her to hurry. When she returned to the gated multi-level stone building at Sulgeneckstrasse 19 that housed the US Embassy, she met him in his office to discuss the situation further.

Her boss, Peter Hyatt, was the case officer in charge of the small team of CIA agents that included Jennifer. There wasn't much spying to do in Switzerland, per se, but gossip and tidbits of information were always drifting in the wind, especially at embassy parties, and sometimes they caught some of it and passed it along to headquarters.

"Could be a crank," Hyatt said. He'd loosened his tie the moment he entered the building that morning. The loosened tie was the only thing sloppy about him. He ran a tight ship otherwise. His worst quality was writing memos, three or four a week—mostly housekeeping items and the other waste-of-time advisories from a boss with not enough to do.

"Aside from the fact that you got lazy and didn't see a civilian following you," he asked, "what do you think?"

Jennifer Turkel didn't argue. She certainly should have spotted Blaser. She *did* regret that her actions would spawn another memo, probably a four-pager on the importance of tradecraft, complete with highlighted excerpts from the field manual.

"It's worth a look."

"The Iranians have their own scientists. Why him?"

"They wanted somebody vulnerable, and they found one," she explained. "I have to file a report anyway. We can't let it go if he's telling the truth."

"Get started. I'll fast-track any requests you have."

Twenty-four hours later, a team flown in from Berlin had Blaser and his family covered with visual, audio, and video surveillance. Jennifer performed the background check from her office.

Seventy-two hours after that, she met with Hyatt again.

"He wasn't lying, and now we're tracking the Iranian, Hamin," she reported. "They're running surveillance on Blaser, too. But they don't want a complete bomb. What they want is a set of krytrons."

"A set of what?"

"The gizmo that actually makes it a nuclear bomb," she said. "Goes in the warhead. It facilitates the atomic reaction. Without krytrons, all you have is a radioactive paperweight. Now that the Iranian deal is dead, they're collecting parts to make up for lost time."

"We have to tell HQ," Hyatt said.

Jennifer and her boss called their headquarters and provided the new information. HQ told them to stand by, and another forty-eight hours ticked around the clock. Then HQ said they had a plan and an agent on the way to implement it.

———

Scott Stiletto arrived in Bern wearing a fancy three-piece suit and carrying a leather-wrapped briefcase.

He didn't mind getting out of his stuffy office for a trip around the world, but he also didn't think he was the right man for the job. He'd said so to his chief, General Ike Fleming, after Fleming explained the situation.

"We're basically running a double agent. That's not my thing."

As an agent with the CIA's Special Actions Division, Stiletto's "thing" was usually dealing with opponents in more direct ways. No, this sort of job wasn't his usual task, but he did have a soft spot for what he called "forgotten victims:" people like Blaser forced into situations out of their control by powerful forces who would kill them if they didn't comply. He liked being the strong opposing force who could dish out the kind of punishment such animals deserved.

Fleming, sitting across the big desk from Scott in his usual dark suit, agreed, but added, "I lobbied for it. The nuclear angle makes it our business, and I think the plan from the seventh floor is a little too fancy. That means risk, and risk means we may need somebody on the ground who can handle such a situation. Our people in Bern aren't exactly in shape for it."

And that meant, Fleming intimated without explicitly saying it, a man of Stiletto's caliber.

Stiletto crossed the tiled floor to where the woman waited. He was tall and well-built, with dark hair and rough hands. Only the hands didn't fit the presentation of a businessman on a trip to Bern. They were a working man's hands.

He introduced himself, but he didn't like the look she gave him. Not everybody on the payroll appreciated the "skull smashers" Scott represented, but the Agency needed them for the special jobs nobody else could handle. He hoped she wouldn't give him a hard time or end up being an appointed hack who couldn't properly do her job.

She led the way to her car, and during the drive, he described the plan.

"You're gonna get that whole family killed," she said.

So much for not giving him a hard time.

"Maybe," Stiletto told her, earning another sharp look, "but only if they do something stupid."

He had no intention of getting anybody killed, but he also wasn't going to bother trying to change her mind. She'd made it up long before he'd arrived. She didn't have to like Scott, but she had to cooperate. The locals were also probably upset that the case was being taken from them, but Scott couldn't help that. Orders were orders.

She brought him to his hotel and returned to the embassy while he checked in. Then he settled down to wait for the nighttime meeting Jennifer had arranged. While waiting, he took out the sketchbook he always carried. He was known around HQ as a very capable artist, having learned the skill as a young Army brat who was always on the move and unable to make friends. He started to draw a copy of a set of photographs supplied by the science section at headquarters.

———

Blaser, as instructed, arrived at a bar not far from the university just before midnight. The lights were low, the walls and carpet dark, and there were flickering candles at every table. He asked the bartender for Mr. Resnick. The bartender directed Blaser to the back room where Jennifer and Stiletto waited. The bar was a CIA front for just such occasions, the walls fitted with countermeasures to foil any electronic eavesdropping. The room was small and bare, but warm. A pitcher of water and three glasses sat on the table. Blaser helped himself to a glass.

The meeting didn't last long, and Blaser did not have much to contribute. The new man did all the talking.

"You will build each krytron," Stiletto instructed him, "to these specifications." He handed Blaser a sheet of paper with a line drawing of a krytron on it, a crude blueprint with notes on one side. He'd drawn them himself.

"But...there are incorrect parts listed here."

"Exactly. That's what you'll give the Iranians."

In return, Stiletto explained, the Blasers would have full protection including around-the-clock surveillance, and the option to move to the United States once the operation was finished. The deal included the choice to work at universities in Southern California or Chicago, where his knowledge of physics would be greatly appreciated, and he'd have the chance to put that knowledge to use on state-of-the-art equipment.

It wasn't the arrangement Blaser wanted. He didn't want to leave his home. But to refuse the Iranians meant death—their threats had been clear —so he had no choice. The scientist agreed and left the bar, the door to the meeting room closing softly behind him.

Jennifer folded her arms. Stiletto waited for her objection.

"What do we do," she said, "when the Iranians discover the ruse and kill the family?"

"We don't let it get that far. Once we have the Iranian network mapped out, we pull the Blasers out and roll up the bad guys."

"You field people are crazy."

"And you sit behind a desk and snoop for gossip at embassy parties, so what do you know?"

"I do more than ride a desk. I shoot expert with the nine-millimeter."

"Ever kill a man?" Stiletto said.

"No."

"Then you don't know what you're talking about."

Her face flushed. Stiletto moved by her and out of the room. He took a seat at the bar and asked for a beer, and felt Jennifer's eyes stabbing through his back.

On the one hand, he had to be cold about the project, but he liked the professor. Anybody who would take the risk of contacting them had to have a reserve of bravery that would make the average man look weak by comparison. When the time came, he wanted to be the agent who took care of that man and his family. He'd make sure he was.

Lars Blaser supplied the faulty krytrons three times a year, delivering each to a dead drop specified by Shahram Hamin, his Iranian handler. Blaser stayed in contact with Jennifer and met with Stiletto on a regular basis.

Agents kept watch over the family and cataloged the Iranian agent, tracing his movements all over Europe and following Hamin to Tehran on several occasions.

Everything went according to plan until Blaser sent an SOS that Scott Stiletto, as he had intended, personally answered.

CHAPTER ONE_

Switzerland – Present Day

TRAVEL the world to hide in an alley. That was the story of his life, Stiletto decided. Sometimes the "alley" was a hole in the desert or some other nook in hostile territory, but the story remained the same.

Stiletto didn't mind, really. He wasn't much of a sightseer. It was a job, and one he wouldn't trade for anything else. Especially this assignment. Blaser needed help, and he had responded without question and come prepared. A Colt Combat Government Series 70 .45 auto with a customized hair trigger for rapid fire hung under Scott's left arm, and his car contained other tools of the trade.

All he lacked was a nice cigar to help kill time, but the scent and smoke from a stogie wasn't exactly part of covert tradecraft.

He stood in the alley between two buildings overlooking the central plaza of a large mall where he was supposed to meet the Blasers for their SOS extraction. The Iranians were onto them. The ruse had been discovered, as had been inevitable once the Iranians actually tried to use the krytrons, and now the CIA needed to get the family to safety. Time to make good on past promises.

Scott shifted his body now and then so as not to get too uncomfortable, but he'd been leaning against the jagged rock wall for two hours. His feet, encased in pair of running shoes, were also tiring of the effort despite the flat concrete ground. Luckily there were no smelly dumpsters or stray cats chasing rodents to distract him.

When Lars had sent the message about needing extraction, Scott had dropped everything and jumped on a CIA plane to Bern. He had visited with the physicist several times over the last few years, cultivating not only a business relationship but a friendship as well. A no-no, for sure, but one thing Stiletto had learned was that you cannot, despite best efforts, turn yourself into a machine, even if you're under orders. It is the nature of humans to form connections, sometimes at a cost, and one must be willing to accept that cost or not truly live. Stiletto figured the world was cold enough already, so one might as well live life to the full.

But that also made this mission *personal*.

Another no-no. Stiletto never went about callously fracturing or ignoring orders and proper protocol, but sometimes it had to be done.

There were so many others Stiletto had not been able to save that, in their names, he needed to go the extra mile for the ones he *could* rescue from the hellfire.

A scratch on the concrete...behind him? Back to the wall, wincing as the rock dug into his spine, he looked at the darkened walkway between the buildings lit by small lamps on the outer walls.

Another scrape...above! Stiletto snapped out the .45 and aimed up as a gunman started to lean over the edge of the roof. One blast turned the top of the assassin's head into a misty red ruin.

Stiletto ran into the plaza. As soon as lamplight hit him, the sub-machine guns started. Stiletto dodged left, then right, then dived into the entrance of a restaurant. He looked back at the roofs of the buildings opposite. The two shooters adjusted their aim and fired at the doorway, shattering the glass behind Scott. He covered the back of his neck as glass rained down, spreading across the ground like spilled water. He fired two more rounds, then a third for insurance. One of the gunners fell back, firing a burst skyward. His partner retreated.

Scott left the doorway, his shoes crunching over the glass, taking deep, steady breaths as he raced along the wall of the building to the west-side parking lot.

A four-door Mercedes screeched around the corner, the surviving shooter leaning out the passenger window.

Scott had four rounds left. He raised it in a two-handed grip and stitched all four across the windshield. Two found the driver and the Mercedes veered away, the shooter gripping the doorframe as his body lurched with the car. Scott reloaded as the car collided with a lamppost, knocking the post over like a chopped tree. The bulbs exploded in a bright flash. The shooter, having been thrown free of the car upon impact, landed on the asphalt face-first a few feet from the car.

Stiletto approached as the shooter started to rise. The man looked at Scott in a daze and the agent shot through the man's head, splitting it open and painting part of the car and the ground with pieces of red flesh and bone bits.

Stiletto ran to his car and started the motor.

He wanted to check the Blaser home before reporting to the embassy. The gunmen at the mall suggested the worst, but what if...

Presently Stiletto switched off the lights and guided the rental to the curb a few doors down from the house. The Blasers owned a single-level at the end of the street with a mix of open space and trees behind the home.

Scott followed the sidewalk. The night's chill dried the sweat on his face. Street lamps lit the way. The houses on either side showed no signs of life at this hour—until he passed one fence and woke a dog. He ignored the barking and strode on. When he came abreast of the Blaser house, he dropped behind a car parked on the street. The dog kept barking. The Blaser house showed as little life as the rest of the neighborhood...until the front curtain moved.

A subtle movement, sure, but the kind of quick check a sentry would make in case the barking signaled the arrival of a rescue team. That meant something in the house might be worth rescuing.

Two vehicles sat in the driveway, one a small passenger car and the other a large SUV. From his dealings with Blaser in the past, he knew that only Blaser's wife drove. Lars biked or used public transit. The SUV was an enemy crew wagon. Scott slid into the shadows on the side of the house and climbed over a gate, the old wood wobbling a little. Landing hard on a concrete path with yard tools to his left, he stayed low and advanced. The Blasers had no pets to disturb.

Darkened windows lined the side of the house. When Scott reached the corner, he stopped and scanned the yard. Swimming pool, garden, some trees. A blaze of light spilled across a portion of the patio, shadows moving across it.

A shovel, a rake, and smaller garden tools leaned on the fence to Scott's right. He put away his pistol and grabbed the shovel, then rounded the corner to see the sliding glass doors that provided a partial view of the family room and adjacent kitchen. A man holding a stubby sub-machine gun focused his attention on the family room.

Stiletto launched the shovel like a spear, throwing high to compensate for the heavy front end. As the shovel arced and began to descend toward the glass, Stiletto hauled out the .45. The metal blade struck the glass low but achieved the desired result. The door shattered, first in the middle, then spider-cracks weakened the rest of the pane. The glass cascaded into the pool of light and the armed man turned with his weapon up. Before he completed the turn, Stiletto detached the gunman's jaw from his face with a .45 slug.

A woman screamed as Stiletto charged through the opening, more glass crunching under him. He swung left, then right. Only Mrs. Blaser and her two kids occupied the family room.

"Where are the others?"

Rubber soles squeaked on the kitchen tile. Stiletto spun and fired at the gunman, who ducked back. The slug tore a hole in the wall.

"Far corner and stay low!" Stiletto snatched the dead man's automatic weapon and jammed the stock into his shoulder. He heard Mrs. Blaser telling her kids to move. Scott watched the kitchen and the hallway to the left that led to the front door and the living room.

The second gunman rounded the corner ahead, attempting to come down the dark hall, but stopped short. Stiletto stitched him from stomach to chest, and the gunman decorated the wall with crimson flecks as he flopped forward onto the carpet.

The blast still stung Stiletto's ears. He moved backward to the Blasers. "Any more?"

They stared at him wide-eyed, the woman holding her young son close on one side and her teen daughter on the other.

"Any more?" he asked again.

The boy held up two fingers.

"Two more, or only these two?" Scott clarified.

"No more, just them," the woman replied.

"Mrs. Blaser, I was supposed to meet you at the mall and get you all out of here. Where's Lars?"

"They took him." Her voice shook.

"Where?"

"The university."

Stiletto grabbed a cell phone from a jacket pocket and dialed.

When Jennifer Turkel answered, he identified himself.

"Cops are all over the mall, Scott!"

"It was an ambush. The Iranians got to them first, but I'm with Blaser's family now." He explained the rest.

"I'm on my way with a tac team."

"Just you and one or two others. They're frightened enough."

"You don't sound like you're staying."

"They've taken Lars to the university. We can't lose him."

"What do you mean, 'Lars?'"

Stiletto hung up.

"Mrs. Blaser, look at me. I need you to listen."

She nodded.

"My people are on the way to get you, but I need to find Lars."

"Go," she said.

"The person coming for you is named Jennifer." He described her. "She'll have some other men with her. You'll be taken to the embassy where it's safe."

The daughter asked, "You'll bring my daddy?"

"You bet, sweetheart. You'll be together soon."

Stiletto ran out to his car.

He drove with hands tight on the wheel. He could not face the family with failure. And that meant he had to rescue Lars Blaser or die trying.

STILETTO KNEW the basic layout of the university from his previous visits.

He parked about a block away and entered the campus on foot, shoulder bag containing various goodies across his back. The physics lab was a small building detached from a larger hall. Scott spotted a sedan and another SUV identical to the one at the house parked near the front door.

He stayed behind a tree and watched for a while. Nobody stood near the sedan, but two men in leather jackets wandered around the SUV, taking turns circling the vehicle and scanning the area.

Stiletto moved his bag to the ground and carefully opened it. He took out a smoke grenade and clipped it to his belt. The Heckler & Koch UMP-45 also inside the bag already had a mag locked and a suppressor on the barrel. An infrared scope sat atop the HK's receiver. Stiletto stowed two more thirty-round mags in his pockets.

He watched the sentries circle the SUV again. Lining up one man in the sights of his weapon, Scott pulled the trigger. The slug hit the sentry low in the neck, splattering the driver's side of the SUV, and the sentry dropped. The other had his gun in one hand and a radio in the other. As he reported the attack, Stiletto shot him in the mouth, the slug opening a hole in the back of the man's head and sending a spray of gore outward. He put down the HK and pulled the pin on the smoke grenade.

The door to the lab opened, and three more gunmen emerged. Stiletto tossed the grenade. As it rolled across the asphalt, thick white smoke spewed, creating a cloud between Scott and the gunmen. Stiletto peered through the scope and lined up the man-shaped heat signatures. The gunmen coughed and called to one another, spreading out. Stiletto triggered short bursts, shifting his aim after each, and the men collapsed. Stiletto left the tree and raced across the space between him and the lab, ignoring the smoke to reach the door. As he ran through it, more gunfire crackled from down the hall. Stiletto dropped flat and fired back, then jumped up and dove through an open doorway. Automatic gunfire peppered the doorway and then stopped.

The room was dark as well, lab tables and stools spread about. Stiletto retreated to a corner. The shooting had come from the left side of the entry hall. He heard two men shouting, and a third man screamed and shouted back. Stiletto recognized the third man: Blaser. At least he was still alive.

But the enemy had Stiletto pinned in place and

outnumbered, and they held the ace. They also couldn't leave via the hallway without crossing his line of sight.

More talking from down the hall. Two more shots smacked the doorway, splintering the frame. Despite his distance from the flying wood shrapnel, Stiletto jumped with each hit. They wanted him to tempt him into making a play for the hallway.

Scott looked around. The windows sure looked wide enough for him to slip through. If he could get to the back door, that might work to his advantage.

He slung the HK across his back and flipped the latch on one window, easing it open, then slipped outside and dropped into a squat among the trimmed hedges alongside the wall. They poked and prodded at him, but provided cover as Stiletto made his way to the corner, around which was the rear door of the building. He stopped to listen. When the lock on the rear entrance snapped and the door opened, Stiletto readied his weapon. They were coming to him—even better. Two men emerged, Blaser and a gunman. A car started around front, and tires squealed. Stiletto fired once. The gunman dropped and Blaser let out a yell, but stopped when he saw Scott. Blaser wiped the gunman's blood spatter off his face and said, "Hamin—"

Tires screeched again as the sedan rounded the corner. The driver, Shahram Hamin, stopped short, tires smoking, and slammed the car into reverse. As the car shot backward, Stiletto fired, but none of the shots connected. The speeding car raced out of range.

Blaser grabbed Stiletto's left arm, almost pulling him down. "He has them! He has them!"

Stiletto shoved Blaser back. "I got your family out of the house."

"No! He has my krytron blueprints!"

Sirens in the distance grew louder as the local police converged.

"We gotta run. Stay in the shadows."

STILETTO AND BLASER slipped away as two police cars pulled up in front of the lab. Back in the rental, Stiletto drove and Blaser caught his breath. As they passed through an intersection, Stiletto said: "I'm sorry I was late."

"I knew you'd come. You said my family is safe?"

"They're at the embassy. That's where I'm taking you."

"He has my blueprints. They made me correct them, so now they can find somebody else. All our work, Scott—it meant *nothing!*"

Stiletto clenched his jaw. There was no argument to reply with.

The only thing they could do was grab Hamin and get the blueprints back. The most important part of the mission, to Scott, anyway, was the safety of the Blasers, and that had been accomplished. Now Stiletto could scorch the earth looking for the man truly responsible for the situation.

JENNIFER TURKEL SAID: "Leaving apartment with briefcase and laptop."

"I see him."

Stiletto's voice reached her via a standard CIA issue com unit with a range of ten miles. She wore the ear bud in her right ear.

Jennifer Turkel had provided another icy reception for him when he arrived twenty-four hours earlier, blaming him and his "Agency cowboys" for the problem, but she had promised she'd do what he told her to make sure the family escaped danger. It was all Stiletto could ask for.

And all he needed her to do was drive the van.

It was the next morning, and Stiletto's team had been watching Hamin's apartment all night. He sat at a table in front of a café across the street from the building, and left the table to blend with the sidewalk traffic as Hamin traveled the short distance to the apartment building's attached multi-level garage. Jennifer rolled up in a black van and Stiletto jumped into the passenger seat. She activated the emergency lights, pressing another button on the dash that stalled the engine. She turned the key and cranked the motor several times as cars behind them stacked up and honked. Stiletto powered down his window and waved them around.

The van looked plain and indeed had no rear seats, but it had reinforced bumpers for ramming. Stiletto's plan called for the use of such a bumper.

When Shahram Hamin exited the garage in his white Mercedes, Jennifer Turkel hit the kill switch again and started the motor. She followed the Mercedes into traffic.

. . .

Iʀᴀɴɪᴀɴ ᴀɢᴇɴᴛ Sʜᴀʜʀᴀᴍ Hᴀᴍɪɴ placed the briefcase and laptop on the passenger seat of the Mercedes. Before starting the car, he opened a panel built into the door near his left knee and checked the Glock-18 machine pistol nestled in the compartment. He had two thirty-two-round magazines inside his jacket.

He didn't wear any old jacket. Hamin liked to travel and live in style. The jacket had set him back $2500—black leather with a silk lining that went with his lightened hair. Style salons were one aspect of Western culture he didn't dislike. His natural black hair had always looked like a dead cat on his head, in his opinion. Properly styled, parted down the middle, and touched with blonde highlights, he looked hip and contemporary.

He started the car and turned on the stereo. The speakers came to life, playing the jazz CD he had picked up on his last trip to the US, steady beats punctuated by a saxophone filing the car. He drove out of the garage.

The shootout at the lab had not been expected and, because of it, the entire network he'd built to smuggle bomb parts into Iran had to vanish. Already fellow agents around the world were pulling out and liquidating loose ends. In the briefcase, he had the corrected blueprints for the needed krytrons. Either Iranian scientists could continue their assembly, or they'd have to find a suitable foreign replacement, appropriately pressured, of course, to do the job.

Hamin's cell rang. "Yes?"

"We're a few cars back," one of his teammates said. "No sign that you're being followed."

"Okay." Hamin hung up.

He knew somebody was back there. Had to be.

STILETTO DIALED HIS SUPPORT TEAM. The other agents used non-descript vehicles to shadow Hamin, rotating every few blocks.

Jennifer stayed as far back as she could to avoid detection.

The second unit called to report that Hamin was heading for the motorway and, more than likely, the airport. Stiletto gave the order. Get lined up to box him in. Standard rendition protocol.

"SHAHRAM, I keep seeing the same two cars."

"I'm almost to the motorway. Stop them."

Hamin put the phone down. As he drove

through an intersection, a black van on his left ran the light and plowed into his front fender with a terrible crash, glass shattering, metal twisting.

The shock of the impact jolted Hamin, but the belt held. The driver's window poured glass bits onto Hamin's lap, but the jazz kept playing as the car spun 360 degrees, tires smoking, the acrid smell of burnt rubber filling the air. The side airbags burst open, and Hamin screamed. The car stopped. Gasping, Hamin felt the side of his face, stung by the impact of the airbag. The skin wasn't cut, but his vision spun. The jazz kept playing. He slammed a palm against the stereo control and turned it off.

He grabbed the Glock-18 as somebody wrenched open the door.

Scott Stiletto leapt from the van with the Colt in hand. Hamin raised a machine pistol, and Scott dropped and rolled. The first burst cut through the air where he'd been, and pain from the impact with the asphalt flared through his body. Hamin fired a second burst into the black van, the bullets smacking the bulletproof windshield but not cracking it. Hamin slid over the hood of his car and took off running. He carried the briefcase along with his gun.

More pistol fire cracked behind Scott, and he rolled over and looked. Two more Iranians were running his way. His support team fired over the hoods of stopped cars, and drivers and pedestrians started screaming, running away if they could. Stiletto jumped up, slid across the Mercedes, and ran after Hamin.

CHAPTER TWO_

HAMIN PUSHED and shoved his way through the pedestrians in front of him. A man grabbed the back of Hamin's jacket, jerking him back, but Hamin swung an elbow and clocked the man in the jaw. Hamin whirled to fire at Scott. The blast missed, and a woman screamed behind Stiletto. Scott stopped at a lamppost and looked back. The woman, bleeding from her arm, clutched at a man, who pulled her to cover behind a parked car.

Stiletto started running again. The situation was deteriorating fast.

He felt his right ear for the com unit, but it had fallen out somewhere during the chase. Pulling out his cell, he called Jennifer, breathing hard as he spoke. "Where are you?"

"One of our guys is wounded, but we took out the other Iranians."

"Get back to the embassy."

Hamin rounded a corner ahead. Stiletto followed, slipping on a patch of wet garbage from an overflowing dumpster and falling hard on his left side. The .45 roared once. Hamin stumbled as the slug blew off the heel of one shoe, but the Iranian agent kept going. He reached the end of the alley and turned right.

Police sirens neared. He was out of options. Stiletto painfully rose, ran to a fire escape in the middle of the alley, and climbed to the roof of the building, the steel groaning under his weight and swaying as he climbed.

HAMIN'S LEGS began to hurt, but he kept moving, walking fast. He'd managed to cover several blocks, but there were still many more to go. He kept looking around, but there was no further sign of the American.

People were out and about, enjoying their evening and paying no attention to him. He slowed as pedestrian traffic thickened, checking storefronts for a specific address.

He spotted the tobacco shop with its Open sign brightly lit.

His government maintained several front operations in major cities around the world, their task to aid any agents who asked for help. Such contacts were made only when there were no other options. Hamin needed a night's rest, transportation, and a secure Skype connection.

The clerk behind the counter watched him expectantly. Hamin figured he looked nothing like a regular customer with the sheen of sweat on his face and the disheveled clothes. He stopped at the counter and spoke a coded phrase in Farsi, and the clerk responded. His expression became interested and serious. Hamin explained the situation and what he needed, and the clerk led him into the back room. It was small and cramped, but it had light and a desk with a laptop. The clerk did not identify himself as he cleared the screen of what he'd been working on and offered the chair to Hamin. He said he'd return with tea.

The room was a back office with some stock stacked in a corner and a small lamp on the desk. Hamin logged onto Skype and connected with his chief in Tehran. Fartosh Pander frowned when he saw Hamin's face.

The Iranian spy chief spoke through a bushy mustache. "Why aren't you on a plane to San Francisco?"

Hamin explained his problem.

"All right," Pander said. "You'll be taken care of tonight, and the brothers will provide you with a car and a new passport. You should probably head for Belgium and get on a plane there."

"Is that smart?"

"The nice thing about going to America is that's where they *won't* be looking for you."

"Something needs to happen to the man chasing me."

"Consider it done, Shahram."

"And you'll tell our contacts in San Francisco that I'll be late?"

"It will be taken care of. Our man there is having some trouble with the final arrangements we need, but he assures me he's taking steps that will permanently solve the problem."

"I'll report when I arrive, sir."

"Good luck."

Pander cut off the feed.

The clerk returned with the tea. Hamin still did not ask the brother's name as they went over what they had to do as a security precaution.

People who remained anonymous couldn't identify each other under interrogation.

The clerk left to return to the counter as a pair of customers entered. Hamin remained in the chair and sipped the tea.

America, the heart of the beast. Hamin had not wanted to argue, but he was wary of working with Americans. The ones who jumped at the chance to make a buck would just as quickly betray him if somebody else offered more money.

But he had his orders, and those orders would be carried out to their fullest extent. Allah help the poor bastard who tried to double-cross him.

Scott sat in the corner of a rooftop till after sunset. The ache in his side caused by his slip and fall had faded. The police search had moved well away from him, and checks over the side showed he was also outside the search perimeter.

What a mess.

The temperature had cooled, and his jacket smelled from the trash he had landed in.

When the sky turned from pink to black, the city lights blazing, he finally worked his way to the street and caught a cab, which dropped him at a restaurant a block away from the embassy.

Scott walked the rest of the way.

Gray clouds and a chill—not the best kind of day to say good-bye to your country.

After a three-day debriefing at the embassy, the State Department had cleared the Blaser family to leave. More agency officials awaited them in the US.

Stiletto drove the van containing the family to the Bern airport, where a chartered jet waited.

Nobody spoke during the drive. The kids were deathly quiet. Stiletto had escorted the family home to collect some belongings, and the kids had fussed indeed about only being able to take a few things. Stiletto knew they'd have a new home with all the trimmings set up by the US government, but of course, it would never match their real home.

Blaser sat up front with Scott. The physicist stared straight ahead. His wife, sitting back with the kids, wore an equally blank stare.

Plenty of speed bumps awaited on the road back to normality, but Scott believed the family was strong enough to prevail.

He turned onto the airport property and pulled into the private hangar where the CIA jet was parked. Scott had ordered it stocked with food and drinks and treats for the kids, as well as a selection of movies to help everyone pass the time during the long flight. Stiletto didn't think any of them would sleep.

Scott and Lars collected the suitcases, and they boarded the plane. The wind rushing into the hangar pushed at their backs.

At least the plane had creature comforts: soft tan carpeting, and leather chairs and couches up against the fuselage. Bathroom and galley in the rear, and a large-screen television up front.

The Blasers tentatively took seats. Scott helped them get strapped in and spoke briefly with the pilot, who said they might shave an hour or more off the flight time if they hit the jet stream.

Twenty minutes later the jet left the runway and climbed through the gray clouds to the blue sky above. The drone of the engines filled the cabin.

Scott served food, and presently the family started to relax. The kids declined a movie, instead playing a board game with their mother.

Lars Blaser sat on a couch opposite his family, hands and knees together, staring at the carpet.

Stiletto sat beside him and handed Lars a beer.

"This is all my fault," the physicist said.

"You can't say that. There were risks from the start. If you hadn't agreed, we wouldn't be talking. They'd have killed you and your family."

"I tell myself that, and wonder if it might have been better that way."

"Lars—"

"Our whole lives have been ripped apart. Do you have any idea—"

"Yes," Scott interrupted. "My pop was an Army colonel, so we moved a lot. Always a new town, school, friends—or not. I kind of stopped making friends after a while."

"You and I became good friends. You came when I called."

"When you only have a few friends," Scott replied, "you do anything for them."

"There is another reason," Blaser prodded. "I can tell."

"There is. I don't like to talk about it."

Lars drank some beer, and finally loosened up and sat back. "I've thought about what you said. How we could pick where we wanted to go."

"Yeah."

"You suggested Chicago or one other place I don't remember, but I like Montana. They have a good university, Montana Technical. It's in an old mining town called Butte."

"Big Sky Country."

"I like the pictures I saw on the Internet."

"Then we'll make Montana your new home," Stiletto assured him.

They fell silent for a while, drinking the beer, and then Blaser said, "They'll find another."

"Not if we round them up first," Stiletto replied.

"When you catch them, maybe we can go back?"

"Don't bet on it. Even if Hamin is taken down, there will be another to replace him, and you can be sure your name is on a list somewhere. They won't forget you."

"Nothing changes," the physicist spat. "It's a never-ending cycle of conflict and violence. You can do nothing but maintain a status quo."

"That's right."

"And this is okay with you?"

"I never said that," Stiletto protested. "If we have the power to change things, we should try. I have the power to do things other people can't, or won't. It's the way of the world, and something I came to terms with long ago. If we can keep the planet from blowing up, maybe the next generation —such as your kids—can finally make it right."

"I wish I didn't know about your life," Blaser said. "I never expected mine to turn out like this." He swallowed another mouthful of beer.

"You can't give up, Lars. Your family needs you now more than ever. You need to reach down deep and lead them through this."

"What if I can't?"

"You will."

"How do you know?" the physicist asked.

"Because you had the guts to come to us in the first place."

Lars Blaser nodded. "I didn't even think about it. I had to."

"Bring that same attitude to your new life, and you'll be fine."

"You can come and visit?"

"I will try," Stiletto said. But it wasn't entirely the truth. Once the Blasers were in full protective custody, he wouldn't be allowed access to their whereabouts.

But at least Lars finally smiled.

San Francisco, CA

IF SHE HADN'T BEEN so busy, Ali Lewis would have had time to count the number of brain cells she had lost due to the *thump-bump-bump* of the EDM blaring from the venue's speakers. Electronic dance music might have been popular, it might have given the models something to walk a beat to, but give her Frank and Dean any day.

You could hardly breathe backstage for all the busyness. Models rushing from one spot to the next, handlers with their ever-present portable communications headsets racing after them, designers hovering and making last-second changes to outfits and complaining about this and that, journalists snooping about. Ali's models, each in a conservative but sexy suit, lined up near the stage door waiting for the crew ahead of them to finish. Music played, and the audience cheered as models walked the runway. As each model came backstage, they returned to their designers' area and changed clothes to go out again.

Ali went up and down the line of her models, making final inspections. She passed along her usual pep talk, trying to massage the nervousness out of their eyes. Every one of them felt it. They stood straight and looked confident, but everybody had a little stage fright just before going out— including Ali, who would have to walk the stage last to either applause or jeers.

It was the last day of San Francisco's Fashion Week. She was showing her new line of work clothes for female tech workers. With so many tech companies making San Francisco home, she wanted to cash in on women who needed smart yet sexy outfits that were also comfortable and fun. No '80s shoulder pads or anything too stuffy. Nothing matronly. No flat colors. A little cheesecake mixed with modesty. She thought she had nailed the concept. The wolves in the audience would tell her.

Sudden boos mixed with the applause and Ali looked out on the stage with concern. A stagehand going by stopped and said, "That rapper and his reality-show wife just showed up."

"They're three hours late!"

"That's why everybody's booing."

Ali went to the edge of the stage to see the couple pushing their way to the front to claim their seats. The rapper wore a black suit, and his TV wife bulged in a tiny dress with her long black hair curled around her shoulders. She towered over him by at least two feet. She waved at a pair of photographers but did not receive any attention in return. Her frown communicated her disappointment.

Ali went back to her models. "Okay, we're next."

More *thump-bump-bump* from the speakers. Ali sent her first model out. The tall blonde marched with hands on hips, offering the audience a smile and wink. Quick turn, back again. Cheers and applause. So far so good. The next model walked out on six-inch heels. Ali finally let out a breath. The crowd wasn't going to devour her just yet.

The next model went out, and the one after that. Ali stayed by the stage watching each walk on the runway, trying to gauge the crowd.

A warm hand fell on her right shoulder, and she turned and smiled. Her father Jay said, "Your mother would be so proud of you, Ali." He'd slicked back his gray hair, and his light cologne was a welcome scent. Ali's nerves quickly calmed at the weight of his hand on her shoulder.

"Long time coming," she said.

The Marla Grace Collection had begun back

in the early '60s when Ali's mother had cashed in on the mini-skirt craze. She followed up with bikinis when demand outmatched supply. Pretty soon, the Lewis family dedicated all their time to the Marla Grace Empire, one line following another with terrific success. Ali finally came on board after her mother passed away a couple of years earlier, and this was the first time she had designed a line on her own.

It was quite a change from her former life at the Central Intelligence Agency.

The wave of models continued, and the crowd applauded. Ali finally allowed a smile to crack the mask. She turned to her father.

"I think we did it."

"*You* did it, honey."

She frowned. "Who's that?"

Jay Lewis followed her gaze through the back-stage crowd.

"Who?" he said. "I don't see anybody special."

"I thought I saw Max Fairmont hanging around."

Her handler announced, "You're next, Ms. Lewis."

Ali's last model made her appearance on the catwalk. More applause. Ali took a deep breath, and her father offered her an encouraging smile. As the young model passed her, Ali ventured onto the catwalk. She smiled broadly. The stage lights nearly blinded her. At least, that way, she couldn't see the faces staring back. When she heard the cheers, applause, and whistles, she grinned. Ali waved, turned, and proudly walked off the stage.

ALI SAT on a folding chair as the clean-up crew swept the backstage floor and erased the rest of the remaining mess. She felt humbled and blessed by the evening's events. There was an after-party waiting for her, and she'd sent her father along first.

She looked around. The backstage lights had been brightened to allow the cleaning crew to see every nook. The bright lights also helped focus her thoughts. Her mother might be proud, she thought. Her father had seemed certain, but Mama Lewis had been the stoic one, her father the extroverted one. Ali was a combination of the two. She tried to take after her father, but her mother was never far behind.

Certainly, though, her mother would have been pleased.

Footsteps behind her.

"Congratulations, Ali."

She stood and turned. Max Fairmont, in a dark suit, hands in his pockets, a smile on his face, stood there. His dark hair was as lush and full as ever, his chiseled jaw making him look like a '30s matinée idol.

"Your mother would be very happy."

"Thank you, Max. I didn't expect to see you here after our last conversation."

Max Fairmont had been an early partner in the Marla Grace Collection, working closely with Ali's mother.

He did have a gleam in his eye, though. The gleam of the entrepreneur. Only those who were like-minded noticed.

He'd quit the Lewis family business in the mid-'70s to start FairSoft, leaving the fashion industry to join the ranks of Silicon Valley software developers.

And he'd approached Ali three times in as many weeks with an offer to buy the company. She'd refused every time.

"I still have connections who got me in the door," he said.

"Well, I appreciate your support."

"I came to make another offer for the company,

Ali."

"My answer hasn't changed."

"I want to buy the Marla Grace Collection. Name a number."

"Oh, so it's 'name a number' this time? Why do you want my company, Max?"

"I know what it is worth, and I'm willing to pay much more."

"I have no number for you."

"At least discuss it with your father. I'm serious about this offer."

Ali shook her head again. "I'll tell him I saw you."

Fairmont let out a sigh of defeat and shrugged. "Well, it's too bad, Ali. Thanks."

Fairmont sauntered away. Ali watched his back, stunned.

ALI TURNED to her father and asked, "Are you sure you have to go back?"

"The work needs to be done, dear. We spent too much time at the party."

"You're gonna be there all night, and you know it."

The older man patted her leg. "After the craziness of this week and today, I have to catch up on other things that didn't get taken care of."

Jay Lewis made a right turn in the company Towncar and continued toward the condo they shared near the Embarcadero. The street was usually so busy during the day you couldn't hear yourself think, but now all was quiet. A glow from the lights at the bus station at the center of the block cast odd shadows on the street. Cars lined the curbsides. The Towncar rumbled over some potholes that never seemed to get fixed. Ali shook her head. For all the wealth in the city, they couldn't keep the streets properly paved.

"That party counted as work, you know," Ali reminded him.

"Maybe for you. I lost count of the interviews you did."

"Because you were chasing women younger than *me*," she exclaimed. "Maybe if you'd been trying to drum up business, you'd be staying home."

Jay pulled up in front of a high-rise condo complex on Harrison. The Bay Bridge loomed in the distance, the trim lights lining every support cable flashing against the dark background of the night sky.

"I'll be back in two hours."

"Nuts," Ali said as she opened the door. "You'll be back when the sun comes up."

Ali's heels clicked on the sidewalk.

She took a key card from her purse.

A man wearing black clothes and a black ski mask lunged from an alcove, grabbing her arm and squeezing hard enough to elicit a cry of pain.

"Daddy!"

The man shoved, and she fell hard on the concrete. Another cry was cut short, pain flooding her backside.

A car door opened and slammed and she heard her father yelling. Feet shuffled on the sidewalk. Men grunted and fists smacked against flesh, the attacker making no noise. Then a pistol cracked.

Dad doesn't carry a pistol!

A body hit the sidewalk with finality next to her. Something wet splashed on her. Feet shuffled again as somebody ran away.

Ali rolled over enough to look, and when she saw the dead eyes of her father staring back at her, she sucked in a gulp of air and let out a scream that echoed up the street.

. . .

HER FATHER WAS D.O.A. She already knew that, and managed to keep it together while a nurse inspected her face. Nothing broken; a bad bruise, and an overnight stay for observation. The nurse left and Ali lost it, pain of a different kind filling her body as she cried into the hospital pillow. The bed creaked as she shifted onto her side.

She eventually stopped, the wet spot on the pillow warming against her cheek. That was when she noticed the police inspector standing beside her bed. Dark hair, light skin, jaw stubble. The only thing he was missing was a cigarette dangling from his lip.

The inspector spoke softly. He understood how difficult it must be, blah blah blah. Just like on tv, but with less meaning. It was a rehearsed line for him. He probably practiced it in front of the mirror before breakfast each morning.

"I'm Danny Clover," he said, notebook and pen in hand. He wasn't the grizzled old-timer she'd have preferred, somebody with experience. They'd sent her a college kid.

"Tell me what happened, Ms. Lewis."

The words came out with little effort. It surprised her. You'd think describing the murder of your father would be tougher. Her throat felt raw and her voice sounded husky, but she didn't stop talking.

Inspector Clover's pen scratched on his notepad and he asked some questions, but he made no promises about catching the killer.

When he left, she lay in bed and realized he also hadn't asked why she was still alive.

She wasn't sure.

Inspector Clover parked his unmarked police car near the start of the street closure and climbed out. A patrolman standing guard lifted the yellow tape for him to pass. He found his men near the entrance. Crime scene techs examined the pools of blood on the pavement.

"Well?"

An inspector named Fitzgerald turned to speak to Clover.

"The camera on the door was disabled, and there were no witnesses. We found a patch of cloth that might belong to the killer's pants, but it's the only piece of physical evidence we have."

Clover scanned the tired faces of the other inspectors, who added nothing. Nobody wanted to be out this late. Especially Clover, but not for the same reason as the others.

"The killer shot the father," Clover stated, "but left the woman alive. Anybody talking to the building manager?"

"Doesn't live here," Fitzgerald said. "He's driving over from Alameda."

"We need to know if this was a botched break-in attempt. If so, have there been others in the neighboring buildings?"

"I'm thinking it was a hit," one of the other inspectors said. "Why let the woman live?"

"If that's where this leads, fine. Otherwise, just work the case and don't speculate," Clover told them.

He gave his men more instructions and returned to his car. As he drove away, he speed-dialed a number on his cell.

"You better have a good reason for waking me, Clover."

"I'll say," said the inspector. "Your man botched it. My guys already think it looks like a hit. The malfunctioning camera doesn't help."

"We may need a scapegoat," the other man told him.

"Something that sews this up would be nice,"

Clover replied.

"I'll be in touch."

"Sweet dreams."

The other man hung up, and Clover put his phone away.

THREE DAYS LATER, Ali unlocked the door to a home she hadn't entered since the murder of her father. The front room felt stuffy. She needed to open a window.

The door shut with a thud that seemed louder than before. Out of habit, she tossed her purse on the chair to the left but then froze.

She couldn't stay here. How could she sleep in this place, knowing she was the only one there?

Ali grabbed her purse, but the phone rang before she could reach the door. She took her cell from the bag.

"Hello?" Her voice shook a little.

Male voice, curt and to the point. "Sell or something worse happens."

The caller hung up.

Ali's whole body shook as she dropped the phone back in the purse. She leaned against the door and took deep breaths, trying not to faint.

CHAPTER THREE_

SCOTT STILETTO SAT at his desk staring at a stack of paperwork and an inbox full of email that he had no desire to deal with. He hadn't bothered to turn on the light when he'd arrived. His side of the building faced the sun, and light streamed through half-closed blinds.

He took his sketchbook from a faded tote bag under his desk, put up his feet, and started drawing from memory the fountain he'd seen in front of a hotel while he was in Bern. To hell with work.

Stiletto sat and sketched steadily for an hour. Growing up with few friends and being constantly on the move with his father's Army assignments meant he needed a hobby he could do alone. Drawing had been the perfect solution. He didn't entertain any thoughts of ever having a professional gallery showing. His pictures were for himself.

The tip of his pen skipped across the paper, creating a vague outline of the fountain. It had been a tiered marble design, with spouts of water flowing down the three levels to the pool at the base. Presently Scott tore the page from the sketchbook, crumpled the paper, and tossed it. The crumpled sheet bounced off the rim of his trash can and landed on the carpet.

His heart wasn't in it, and he was upset about the Blaser job, too. Some things couldn't be helped, but Scott figured there had been two or three other options open to him during the Hamin chase that he didn't take. Of course, it was all in his head. He couldn't name what those options might have been. The failures always stuck with him. He could barely remember the successful missions most of the time.

Turning his chair to look out the office window, ignoring the blinds in the way, he sat with his lips in a flat line and his jaw tight.

At least the Blaser family was safe.

When his office door opened and his department secretary entered, he turned. She stopped short.

"You don't look happy," Judy Kragen said. She was a middle-aged mother of three who had trained at the Farm with Scott.

"I'm not."

"This arrived for you." She held out an envelope. "Fresh from the x-ray."

"Doesn't anybody use e-mail anymore?" He took the envelope but didn't force a laugh. Judy departed and closed the door.

His frown turned to concern as he opened and read the letter.

SCOTT,

I don't have an email for you, and for all I know you've quit the Agency, but I have nobody else to turn to. Jesus, did I just write that? My father has been murdered, and I know who did it. I have no proof, and the police think it was a random crime, so they're no help. I know I'm asking a lot, but can you come to San Francisco and at least listen to my story?

Ali.

. . .

SHE HAD SIGNED her name with an enlarged, exaggerated A. Some things never changed. His pulse raced. He was surprised that just seeing her name gave him such a reaction. Then again, he had loved her once.

He put the letter down, picked up his phone, and dialed an extension.

David McNeil, General Ike's chief of staff, answered on the third ring.

"It's me," Scott said. "I need to see the boss."

"He's booked for the day."

"Tell him Ali Lewis is in trouble. Her father's been murdered."

"Oh, no," McNeil exclaimed. "I'll tell him now. Hold on."

Stiletto waited for two minutes.

"He'll see you right now."

ALI LEWIS HAD PRECEDED McNeil as Ike Fleming's chief of staff, holding the position for four years before leaving to help run her family's clothing design business in San Francisco. She and Scott had dated for part of that time.

General Ike read the letter with his glasses perched on the edge of his nose. He sighed with fatherly concern and put the letter down. "What a shame."

"Yes, sir."

"What is she expecting?" General Ike said. "This is a police matter. We can't possibly get involved."

Stiletto shifted in his chair. "I can take some time off."

"And do what?"

"See an old girlfriend."

"Uh-huh."

"I don't know what Ali wants other than to talk to somebody who might actually listen," Stiletto said. "I still have a pal at the San Francisco FBI office. Maybe I can be a go-between for her."

"Maybe you should just call and refer her to him."

Scott said nothing

"Her tale of intrigue is too much to resist," the general added. "Let's not kid ourselves about that. You may go as a close friend and concerned citizen, but I know I don't have to remind you about the law, or taking risks that will expose you or the Agency."

"Of course."

"Have a good trip."

Stiletto nodded and started for the door.

"Scott?"

"Yes, sir."

"Give her my condolences."

Scott nodded and let himself out of the office.

STILETTO TOOK the long way home because he enjoyed driving his car more than any other activity. The car was a 1978 Trans Am, bright red, which he had rebuilt and restored with great care. The new paint job had eradicated the original "screaming chicken" on the hood. He'd also updated the car with a heavy-duty suspension that provided exceptional cornering abilities that the factory setup had lacked. As a final touch, he had rebuilt the 454-cubic-inch engine so that the 310-horsepower plant carried the car along at a rocketing pace.

His cell phone rang. He clicked the answer button, holding the wheel with his left hand. "Yes?"

"Agent Stiletto, this is Corporal Argo at the Security Desk. Sir, your home alarm has been triggered."

"That's not good."

Agency employees with top secret and above clearance had alarms installed at their homes that alerted Agency security personnel in case of a break-in. Local police were also informed. Agency men usually made it to the scene first to make sure occupants were okay and nothing sensitive had been stolen.

"I have a security officer on his way to assist you, and have notified the police."

"I'm just around the corner, so I'll be there in a second."

"Sir, that's not wise—"

Stiletto ended the call and dropped the phone on the passenger seat.

Two minutes later he pulled up in the driveway, and the car rocked forward as he stomped the brakes. His house sat on the corner of the cul-de-sac, adjacent to the street. A woman stood in the doorway. Her open-mouthed expression showed she wasn't expecting Stiletto either.

Before Scott even had his seatbelt off, the woman whipped up a Heckler & Koch MP-7 and let fly with a long full-auto burst that ripped into the car.

Stiletto flung himself across the center console and passenger seat. The gear shift dug into his

stomach, and he bumped his head on the glove box.
His legs remained twisted under the wheel. The
windshield popped, and glass rained down; Stiletto
covered his neck, but a shard of glass pierced his
cheek. He'd seen enough of the MP-7 to note the
long fat snout at the end, a silencer.

He'd seen the woman, too: long dark hair,
tanned skin, wearing a trim white pantsuit and
pink scarf. Assassin chic.

Stiletto stretched across the passenger seat
and yanked open the door. He shinnied over the
center console using his elbows, bashing an ankle
on the steering column. Another stream of MP-7
fire cut into the car and Stiletto cursed as his
hands and knees met the rough driveway. He tore
the Combat Government from its shoulder
holster and fired twice over the hood. His gun
wasn't silenced, and the loud blasts filled the air.
The woman ducked into the doorway. He
crawled for the rear bumper, keeping low; she
fired some more, but the string cut short. Out of
ammo.

Stiletto fired over the trunk, and the woman
yelped. Stiletto fired again and again, and half-rose
to rush the porch when his opponent dropped a
canister which hissed out a cloud of white smoke.

Soon the smoke concealed the open door, and the woman as well.

Stiletto sprinted around the side of the house. He grasped the top of the rickety back gate, vaulted it, and raced down the short passage to the backyard, evading pieces of stray yard equipment and cursing his lack of organization. He reached the corner, stopped, and took aim. The woman, at the fence facing the street, tossed over the MP-7 and began hauling herself up. Stiletto's first short splintered the fence near her right hand, but she didn't stop, just swung one long leg over the top. Stiletto fired again—another miss—and the slide of his autoloader locked back over the now-empty magazine.

The dark-haired woman rolled over the top of the fence, and a string of slugs splintered the wood as she fired from the other side.

Stiletto ran back down the passage to the driveway while slapping a fresh mag into the .45. He pulled the gate release, leaving it open, and madly sprinted across the front yard. An engine revved, and tires screeched. Stiletto reached the other side of the house to see the woman half in a blue sedan parked on the curb. The car sped away.

Stiletto aimed at the departing sedan but held

his fire. Despite the .45's high-visibility sights and national match barrel, he wasn't one hundred percent sure that a hit at this distance would do any good.

Sirens on their way. Neighborhood dogs barked. Stiletto had to stand his ground. One look at his car told him he wasn't going anywhere.

He jammed the .45 back under his arm and went to the porch, coughing. The smoke screen had begun to dissipate, and he entered. Not heavily furnished, the house looked like a plain bachelor pad because it was. His. He had just moved in, so there were a lot of boxes stacked along the walls. He'd finally given up his Manassas apartment, mostly so he could have a garage for the now-shot-to-hell Trans Am.

The sirens grew louder. Stiletto scanned each room. No sign of other killers. Who else had been in the blue sedan, and how long until he saw them again? Had the Iranians sent them?

Stiletto returned to the front of the house. He had only a moment to give his Trans Am a heart-broken glance, but then his thoughts turned to the arriving police. The squad cars halted. The first cop out leveled a shotgun and told Stiletto to freeze.

He put up his hands.

THE OLDEST OF the four officers, a white-haired sergeant, kept Stiletto covered while his younger partner did the frisking. The two backup cops stood with shotguns and looked mean. The frisker, a young man with black hair cut above his ears, tugged out Stiletto's .45 and his wallet. He stepped back as if Stiletto were a hot stove. The cops with the guns tensed their shoulders. They didn't blink.

"In my wallet, you'll find my identification. I am a federal officer."

The white-haired sergeant lowered his weapon and looked at the Homeland Security ID the younger officer held up. He ordered his men to lower their weapons.

"What happened here?"

"This is my house, and somebody just tried to kill me," Scott said. "A representative of my department will be here to answer questions."

"You can't—"

"I can."

Presently the Agency security officer, a clean-cut young man, arrived and told Stiletto to report back to the general. Stiletto left in the Agency car, a four-door Chevy without air conditioning or stereo. A cleaning crew would arrive soon to take care of the wrecked Trans Am and the rest of the damage. He'd think of rebuilding the car later. Stiletto sped away from the neighborhood with his hands tight on the wheel.

He arrived at General Ike's office and the general rose to his feet, concern flooding his eyes.

"You're hurt."

"Huh?"

"Your face, Scott."

Stiletto touched his face and saw blood on his fingertips.

"Glass, sir."

"Tell me." The general motioned to the seat in front of the desk and Stiletto related the story.

When Scott finished, the general said nothing for several moments. He made a tent with his hands.

"Hamin?"

"More than likely," Stiletto said. "He got a good look at me in Bern."

"What about your car?"

"I'll rebuild it."

"I know how much you enjoy that vehicle."

"I could use a ride to the airport."

"Take an Agency car. I'll send somebody to collect it later." The general opened his desk drawer and took out a bottle of Tylenol. That meant one of his migraines was hammering at his skull. He swallowed the pills with the ever-present glass of water on the left side of the desk blotter. The headaches always showed up when the pizza hit the fan.

"I'll be in touch, sir."

Fleming nodded, and Stiletto exited the office.

As soon as Scott hit traffic, the blue sedan fell in behind him. Stiletto pulled his pistol from shoulder leather and jammed it under his leg. He drove straight for a while, keeping an eye on the sedan. He had a score to settle. Might as well settle it with Hamin's goons. The blue sedan remained behind and one lane over.

Stiletto called General Ike.

"The shooters are following me."

"We shouldn't waste an opportunity for interrogation," the general said. "I'm sending back-up. Is your tracking device on?"

Stiletto said, "Yes" and reached under the dash, ripping out a set of wires. "It's on." He tossed the wires on the passenger-side carpet. Stiletto put away his phone. Traffic was too thick for him to outrun the assassins. Off to his left, across the opposing lanes, was a shopping center, and he cut over and stepped on the gas. He entered the parking lot, and the car jolted over a speed bump.

Stiletto kept up his speed as he rolled behind the grocery store. He identified a few parked cars, scattered pieces of garbage, and a pair of dumpsters, but there were no people to get in the crossfire. He jammed on the brakes, threw the car into Park, and jumped out with his gun in his hand.

The assassins in their blue sedan turned the corner, and the tires screeched as the car stopped. The driver twisted the wheel for a getaway U-turn and Stiletto fired. Two slugs punctured the glass, and two more turned the driver's face into a pulpy red crater. He slumped over the wheel and the car moved forward at idle speed, executing a slow turn. The woman in the passenger seat opened her door and rolled out before Stiletto finished his fourth shot, but Stiletto tracked her and fired again and again. The bullets pinned the woman to the ground, where she stayed, legs stretched out, MP-7 in her left hand. Her pantsuit was stained red front and back. The rolling car clunked into a dumpster and stopped.

Stiletto jumped back into his car and took off. His cell phone rang, but Stiletto turned it off. He kept driving.

CHAPTER FOUR_

STILETTO LANDED AT SFO, signed for a rental car, and drove north on Highway 101 to San Francisco, guided by the GPS in his phone. The car was a slate-gray Chevy Cruze that looked large outside but was cramped inside. The steering wheel blocked a portion of the speedometer because he had to raise it up all the way to keep the wheel from rubbing against his knees. Luckily a secondary digital speedometer made up for that.

He had to focus on the traffic in front of him since the roadway curved here and there, never going straight for long, but he kept stealing glances at the bay off to the right. It was a crisp blue against the equally blue sky. He could have used the off-road pullouts to enjoy the sight a little longer, but it was best to stick to business. The Cruze seemed like a good car, but it wasn't his Trans Am. It was just another modern car that basically drove itself and was primarily designed for driver comfort instead of fun, which made it lifeless and uninteresting.

Stiletto wanted his Trans Am back in a big way and let his mind work on how he might accomplish the goal. He exited off the 280 extension, turned right on Brannan, and crossed an intersection to stop at a corner tavern. There was something else on his mind, too, forcing out thoughts of the car. Inside, he ordered a Maker's Mark on the rocks and sat at the bar. He wasn't the only one there.

He wasn't ready to see Ali yet.

Scott leaned his elbows on the bar and looked at the amber liquid in his glass. He had joined the CIA after retiring from the Army with the rank of major. His significant experience in special operations had opened up several options in the civilian security industry, and he'd been set to take one of those jobs when his wife, Maddy, died from cancer. The double blow of his daughter Felicia suddenly wanting nothing to do with him and not explaining why left Stiletto adrift. That was when he decided to go back to government service and joined the CIA.

About a year into his Agency employment, during a hike organized by some CIA staffers, Stiletto had met Ali. They had forged a quick connection when they realized they worked in the same department. It had been a little awkward when she took over the chief of staff role. They'd been worried the higher-ups would disapprove, but nobody had objected to their relationship, so they kept it going but remained low-key around headquarters. They'd enjoyed a couple of years together before everything unraveled. He thought about the last thing she had said to him on their final night together:

"You're not here with me. You're somewhere else, and I can't stand lying awake at night wondering if you're coming back this time. I can't do it anymore."

And with that, she broke off their relationship. Six months later she moved to California to work with her father who, ironically, now lay dead by another man's hand.

He hadn't tried to reason with her that night. He could, of course, have transferred to an office assignment, but his physical absence had not been what she referred to. He was mentally absent because he felt guilty about cheating on his late wife, and no amount of mental gymnastics navigated him around such an irrational thought. But just because it was irrational didn't mean the thought didn't exist. He didn't have the feeling after the occasional fling, which meant nothing to him, but with Ali, he was trying for something more. He was trying to rebuild what he'd lost, and it was too much to ask.

Now Ali needed help. She was one of the forgotten victims he visualized so often, those without a champion who needed one. Those under the oppression of a great force that needed a greater force to balance the scales.

Scott finished his drink and returned to the rental. He had wanted to sort out his thoughts, but instead departed more confused than when he'd arrived.

STILETTO CHECKED in at the Hyatt off the Embarcadero.

He stood at the room's window overlooking a view of the city, which offered lots of high-rise buildings. If he looked left, he could see the Bay

Bridge stretching across the bay. It was a bridge, nothing special about it. Gray, drab, a steel-and-concrete monstrosity. He'd seen a million of them. The Embarcadero below, the major roadway that ran along the waterfront, was very busy, vehicles overflowing the two lanes on either side of a dividing island that doubled as a track for underground trams.

He turned from the window and picked up the phone, then dialed Ali's number and took a deep breath as it rang.

"Hello?"

"It's Scott. I'm in town."

"Oh my God, Scott, can you come over now?"

"Sure."

"Where are you staying?"

He told her.

"You're only a few blocks away. I'll send a car over."

How fancy.

He told her he'd be ready and hung up. As he put the phone down, he wasn't sure how he felt about hearing her voice again. It surprised him that he really didn't feel anything at all.

. . .

SHE ANSWERED the door dressed in black, but her eyes flashed when she looked at him. She didn't fight a smile as she invited Scott inside, and gave him a weak hug. Her slim frame felt fragile to him. She'd always felt fragile.

"How was the ride?" she asked.

"Okay. Lots of traffic."

"Always, in this town."

"Nice place," he said, glancing around the living room. Everything looked expensive, but nothing looked like anybody really lived there. The counters and floor were spotless, the furniture perfectly aligned. It might as well have been a display home.

But enough of that, he decided. He looked at Ali.

"We were all stunned by your letter. The general sends his condolences."

"How is the old goat?"

She started across the living room to the kitchen, and he followed. She handed him a beer from the fridge, and they sat on the balcony. She had a terrific view of the bay and the Bay Bridge. Noise from the span wasn't too loud. Fog drifted in from the Golden Gate, and with it came a chill. Stiletto felt the chill up his neck. How much was the fog to blame?

"He's doing well," he said, "and currently upset with me for some unpleasantness over my last assignment."

"Wish you could say more."

"Enough of that. I didn't come here to talk about me."

Her gaze lingered on the bay. A cargo ship sailed under the span of the bridge, and smaller sailboats sliced across the water.

"You can smoke if you want."

"I didn't bring any cigars."

"There's a tobacco shop a few blocks away you might like."

"Ali."

Her voice cracked. "It all happened so fast."

She held it together while explaining the murder, drawing on the strength built up over years of tense moments in General Ike's office.

"What did you mean about the cops?"

Ali threw up her hands. Her voice became stronger as frustration flooded her face. "Random crime. Somebody will try and make a deal someday and they'll name the shooter, but they have nothing to go on.

"There should have been a video of the attack, but somebody deactivated the lobby cameras."

"The shooter wore a mask, you said."

"Doesn't matter. Those cameras should have been working. Maybe one might malfunction, but all of them?"

"You think this was a hit."

"Yes," Ali said.

"Why?"

"One of my mother's original partners, Max Fairmont, left to start a software business. We only communicated through Christmas cards. Then, all these years later, out of the blue, Max offers to buy the company for more than it is worth. Three or four times he tried to get me to sell, but I kept telling him no. Then Dad gets shot, and the day I got out of the hospital, somebody called me and said, 'Sell, or something worse happens.' I can't imagine what, though."

"Have you told the cops?"

"About a crank call?"

"I suppose they'd say that," Scott said.

"I don't know what kind of stuff Fairmont gets mixed up in, but who else? The only thing that doesn't make sense is why he would resort to *murder* just to buy a company."

Stiletto drank and watched the tanker in the bay. The slow-moving vessel had cleared the span. Tug boats chugged their way toward it to guide the tanker into port.

"Can you help, Scotty?"

He shook his head and related his chat with General Ike prior to his departure.

She sank in her chair. "I knew you were going to say that. I don't know what I was thinking." She drank some beer. "Don't you still have an FBI contact out here?"

"Toby O'Brien, yeah."

"Well, maybe—"

"We'd have to show he has a reason to get involved," Scott said. "If it remains a local police matter, his hands will be tied."

"How do we find that reason?"

"I'll do whatever I can, but if you're expecting—"

"No, not at all. I just needed somebody to listen. And help a little. Jesus, Scott—" She finally choked, set down the beer, and started to cry.

Scott went over to her, and she stood up. They embraced. Despite the chill from the fog, she felt warm against him. He held her while she sobbed on his shoulder.

CHAPTER FIVE_

It took two days, but Stiletto finally picked up Inspector Clover's trail. The inspector sat down for lunch at an outdoor café near the Ferry Building, the domed clock tower on top of the building casting a shadow on the street. Stiletto pulled over an extra chair and showed Clover his hands. Two seagulls flapped overhead.

The inspector, a bowl of steaming chili before him and the spoon halfway to his mouth, kept his left hand under the table.

"I'm a friend of Ali Lewis," Scott said. "Don't want any trouble. I just have some questions."

"It's lunchtime."

"She's been calling you."

"I have many cases to deal with, many people calling. I can't spend all day on the phone."

"Inspector—"

"Your friend is the victim of a random crime. We have a lot of those in this city."

"Sounds like all you've done is file a report."

"I've done a hell of a lot more than that." Clover raised his voice, but the nearby traffic and pedestrian noise drowned out most of the indignation. He lowered it again as he spoke. "You probably wouldn't understand."

"What if I told you I think it wasn't random at all?"

"You watch too many movies."

"The disabled lobby cameras weren't a clue?" Stiletto asked.

"We found repair guys in the basement pulling an all-nighter to get them fixed. Look, it was a botched robbery attempt, okay?"

"Really?"

"Ms. Lewis's father managed to tear off the shooter's pants pocket, and we found a list of things he wanted from a specific home. That's it. End of story."

"And we're back to you just filing a report."

"I know within the next couple of months,

we'll bust somebody on another charge and he'll give up the shooter to make a deal. Happens all the time."

"Ali told me you'd said that to her."

Stiletto kept his eyes on Clover. The inspector put down his spoon and leaned forward.

"Word of warning. I know a military man when I see one."

"Ex."

"Still recent. Stay out of trouble, or I'll be locking you up."

"'Cause a previous administration said us military types are a problem, aren't we?"

"You can be."

"Especially in this city?"

"What does that mean?"

"I know a leftie cop when I see one."

Clover clenched his jaw.

"Careful not to wear out your ass from sitting too much," Stiletto advised. He stood and walked away, but glanced back to see Clover's smoldering eyes following him. He waved.

CLOVER WATCHED Stiletto climb into a cab, then scowled at the chili. He didn't have an appetite anymore. He took out his phone and made a quick call.

"I just had a visitor."

"We know."

"What?"

"The woman has called for help. We're on him. Relax and carry on."

Clover ended the call and tried to finish his lunch, but it was cold.

STILETTO GAVE the cab driver the address of a restaurant uptown and glanced back periodically as the taxi moved through traffic. He ignored the odd smell in the back of the cab and the vomit stain on the plastic partition between him and the driver, although he wondered if the stain was the cause of the smell. He decided not to ask. Instead, Stiletto watched a sedan that stayed with them, keeping a discreet distance back. The driver not changing lanes or turning another direction over the same three-block distance as the cab wasn't a coincidence.

Stiletto carried no weapons, but if Ali was right and Max Fairmont was attempting a different kind of hostile takeover, he couldn't very well refuse the lead, along with a chance to strike back and show Fairmont he had a new obstacle.

The cab stopped for a light. The meter read $20. Stiletto tossed forty dollars onto the front seat and bolted from the vehicle, running up the sidewalk to an alley.

He flattened against the right wall and waited. The cement was cracked, with debris strewn about. He'd need to watch his step if the hand-to-hand went on too long. A shadow grew on the sidewalk. The man who entered the alley wore street clothes and a light jacket. He had his hand on a holstered pistol. Young, wiry, and not fast enough.

Stiletto snatched off his sunglasses, the man wincing at the sudden surge of light. Stiletto grabbed his gun arm and twisted, then flung his opponent against the opposite wall. The man struck back with a swing that connected with Scott's jaw. Stiletto ignored the flash of pain. The man charged, but Stiletto met him with a one-two solar plexus strike. As the man sucked air, Scott grabbed an arm and flipped the man over his back, slamming him to the pavement. That was it. Good night, Irene.

Scott quickly searched the man's pockets. Ignored the gun. Found a cell phone. No car keys.

Scott ran back to the street. Dude had left his car in the middle lane. Other cars stacked up behind it, angry drivers jerking their cars around the unoccupied vehicle. Stiletto endured honks and four-letter words as he hopped behind the wheel and drove away.

At the next light, he dialed the last number called on the assailant's phone.

"Where is he now?" a voice on the other end said.

"Knocked out in an alley," Stiletto said. "But I think you mean me. I'm in your guy's car. Y'all are going to have to do better than that. This is a man's game, and you're fielding children."

"Just you wait, Mr. Hero."

The line went dead, and Stiletto put down the phone. He laughed. He'd been called worse.

"What do you mean, they attacked you?"

"Just one."

"Still," she said.

Ali had chosen a restaurant with outdoor seating that Stiletto did not like. He did not want to be so exposed right now. He looked around as they ate. Plenty of people, not only in the seating area but on the sidewalk. They provided some natural cover, but Scott still didn't like it. He didn't like the hard chair he was sitting in either. It made his rear end hurt.

Ali had ordered a chicken salad, while he munched on fish-and-chips.

He told her more of what happened after the fight.

"Was that smart?"

"It proves your theory. Your father's murder was no random crime."

"So now what?"

Another man approached the table. Dark suit, no sunglasses. Heavily built, mostly muscle. When the man spoke, Scott recognized his voice from the cell phone exchange.

"Ms. Lewis."

"What do you want, McCormick?"

Stiletto rose from his chair, the metal legs scraping on the concrete as the man called McCormick reached into his coat.

"Relax, Mr. Hero," the other man said. He handed Ali an envelope.

"What do I do with this?" she said.

"Open it."

Ali instead tore it in half and set the pieces on

the table.

"Tell Max to go to hell. If you think for one second—"

"Fine, then." McCormick started to leave.

"Hey," Scott called.

McCormick turned.

"See you soon."

"We'll have fun, I'm sure."

McCormick moved away.

Stiletto sat again and resumed eating.

Ali picked at her salad.

"You okay?"

She kept her eyes down.

"Hey."

She looked up at him.

"We're going to find out what's behind this and stop it, I promise."

She didn't respond right away, but her eyes scanned his face. Finally, she said: "I believe you."

McCormick DIDN'T HAIL a cab but walked instead, thinking. He still had an hour or two before Fairmont finished a meeting with his development staff. He couldn't report until that ended.

He picked up a *Motortrend* and a bottle of

Evian at a corner store and walked up the block to Union Square. He found a bench where he sat to read and think, especially about the new problem. Pigeons waddled over but lost interest when they realized he had no food for them.

Their research on Ali Lewis hadn't pointed to anybody with a cowboy complex. Whoever Mr. Hero was, he had come at first call. What was the connection between them? Old boyfriend? Certainly nobody recent, and why would an old flame come to her aid? He wasn't just anybody. He was certainly not afraid to fight.

Clover had mentioned he was military. Ali had never served in the military, so he ruled out a connection there.

Who *was* Mr. Hero?

McCormick decided the heck with it and focused on reading. Fairmont wasn't finished with his plan. That meant Mr. Hero would be around for a good long while.

MAX FAIRMONT, at the head of the conference table, stood as the last of the software staff concluded their updates. Somebody coughed.

"Thanks, everybody," he said. "I'm very

pleased with the progress. Pleased enough to say I want a full demonstration of the system ready for the SalesForce show in two weeks."

He hadn't taken off his black suit jacket, which matched his thin tie. The grin started to fade a bit. It was tougher and tougher to keep up the façade lately. His company wasn't what it used to be. Once one of the leading tech celebrities in the Bay Area, he was now an also-ran.

His company, FairSoft, was probably not going to survive the next twenty-four months. He had a plan for his next move, but that damn woman wasn't cooperating.

He glanced at the pensive faces around the table.

"No bugs, either," Fairmont said. "Come on, should be easy." He clapped his hands twice. "Get busy. Two weeks!"

He sat down as the staff filed out. They'd cuss and grumble, but the product would be ready on time. When the last person exited, McCormick slipped in and joined Fairmont at the table.

"Well?" Fairmont said.

McCormick talked about Mr. Hero for almost ten minutes. Fairmont checked his watch once McCormick stopped talking.

"I got a tee time." He stood.

"Are you kidding, Max?"

"This is the stuff I pay *you* for," Fairmont said. "Besides, I'm playing with Rollins. He'll want to know what you've told me."

Fairmont exited and left McCormick alone.

MAX FAIRMONT HAD NOT COME this far to be derailed by anybody.

He *needed* Ali's company. The deal with the Iranians depended on it, and he was under no illusion that they'd let him live if a problem developed.

He'd experienced his first entrepreneurial venture as a youngster when he took on a paper route to earn money for a bicycle. After that, he knew he had to be in charge of his own destiny, and Ali's company was an important part of that destiny.

Fairmont crossed the Golden Gate Bridge into Marin County and soon pulled through the gates of the San Geronimo Golf Course. The rolling greens spread out before him.

He found Peter Rollins, an associate who'd introduced him to the Iranians, in the pro shop. The taller, light-haired Rollins stood in a back corner examining a new set of clubs. He replaced a driver on the rack when he saw Fairmont approach.

"I thought you might be late," Rollins said.

"Been hearing things?"

"Just what the blue jays whisper."

They bypassed caddies to the dirty looks of the youngsters standing ready, and decided to skip a golf cart as well. Birds chirped, and the chatter of other golfers drifted past on the light wind. It was a great day for golf. No clouds, and even the wind didn't pose a problem. The links were as lush and green as ever. Fairmont loved the course. There was no better place to relax. He didn't even mind talking business, which was why he and Rollins played a few rounds and, indeed, talked business once a week. No matter what was happening, Fairmont stayed cool as long as he was swinging.

Their small talk ceased as they knocked their first balls onto the fairway. Once on the green, Rollins brought up business.

"I was against killing the father to begin with," he stated.

Rollins putted for the hole but his ball curved at the last moment, stopping just shy of the cup.

"Worse, Ms. Lewis called for help."

"I have McCormick gathering info on the help." Fairmont tapped his Statinger 7 and it rolled right into the hole. He retrieved the ball with a grin.

"But, Max—"

"We're in no danger. Everything is covered with the cops."

They moved on to the second tee.

"Our friends won't like it if that changes," Rollins said. He placed his ball on the tee and prepared his swing. "I talked to Clover about a scapegoat." He swung, and the ball flew upward in a curve, landing midway down the fairway. "Ms. Lewis wants justice. Let's give her some."

"A sacrifice?" Fairmont addressed his ball.

"Doesn't have to be one of ours."

"I'm not sure about that," Fairmont said.

"If they stop poking around, that makes our project easier."

"Problem is, we're running out of time. We need to get rid of Mr. Hero and not hurt the woman. Take away her options and she'll fold."

Fairmont swung but sliced. His ball went high and angled into the rough.

"Tough luck, Max," Rollins said.

CHAPTER SIX_

THE LAUNCHER SPAT a baseball and the batter
swung, the solid wood bat smacking the ball back
where it came from. The man who held the bat
had removed his tie and unbuttoned the top of his
shirt, but his attire screamed exec and clashed with
the jeans and T-shirts of everyone else on the
batting line.

Stiletto watched the man whack another ball
into the backstop and then made his approach. Up
and down the line he heard the launch of baseballs,
bats striking balls, and the backstop impacts.
Chunk, whack, splat, a soundtrack punctuated by
excitement or disappointment as balls landed on
target or flew foul.

The man took up the ready position with the

bat over his shoulder in a firm grip. *Chunk, whack, splat.* Bull's-eye again.

"Do you ever miss?"

The man turned and smiled. "Wondered when you'd come around."

"How did you even know I was in town, Toby?"

The man pressed a button on the wall of his booth that turned off the launcher and used a towel to dry his face.

"You entered the state under your own name, buddy. That set off an alarm."

Toby O'Brien was a special agent with the FBI and a close friend of Scott's from their Ranger days. He had played a crucial role in Stiletto's previous assignment across the bay in Berkeley. They shook hands, and O'Brien said he had another ten minutes on his "work out," so Stiletto stepped back while the G-man finished swinging.

"We'll beat the DEA for sure this year," O'Brien said later, his shirt and tie restored, as they walked outside to join the sidewalk crowd and traffic noise. They passed a bus stop where two homeless men argued about whether the earth was flat, and stopped at a coffee shop on the corner.

O'Brien held the door for Scott. They sat near the back.

O'Brien didn't have as many lines on his face as Stiletto, but they were the same age. O'Brien was a little shorter and fair-skinned. Rumors existed that he dyed his hair to remove its natural red. Those rumors were false, but O'Brien thought it was funny.

A waitress brought their drinks. Coffee with sugar for O'Brien. Stiletto had green tea with lemon.

"What's up?" the FBI man asked.

Stiletto explained the case so far.

O'Brien let out a sigh. "That's awful."

"Does the Fairmont name mean anything to you?"

"Oh, yes," the Fed replied. "I'd like to ask him a few questions. I wouldn't put what you describe past the man, but proving it will be the challenge. Fairmont seems like another high-tech junkie with lots of bling, but behind the scenes, he's as dirty as can be."

"How?"

"All supposition, of course," O'Brien said. "The company produces products and hires people and pays taxes and all that, but when I worked

OrgCrime, I watched Mr. Fairmont grow chummy with a man named Jimmy Califano. Local syndicate boss. We think Fairmont launders Califano's money."

"Really?"

"They met at a big party in North Beach. Met honestly enough, but as time went on, they talked more and more. We never had enough to show they were anything more than drinking buddies.

"It was about six months after that party that the DEA lost track of Califano's drug money. That gave us the idea that he was using Fairmont instead of regular means. Made it totally invisible."

"Why would he want Ali's company?" Stiletto asked.

"Word is that Fairmont is losing his grip on the computer world. Their last few software releases haven't done well, so they need to score with the next one or they're history. Ali, however, is going strong."

"Could be."

"Do you have another guess?"

"Not right now." Stiletto sipped his tea. It warmed him inside. "What you need is a whistle-blower."

"We had one, once, almost. A woman who

worked for Fairmont and also dated him. She came forward, but—"

"Died before she could talk."

"Yup. An inspector named Clover worked the case. Now there's a tough nut. Wouldn't help an old lady cross the street. He arrested somebody for the murder, but I've always figured the guy was a ringer. Died in a prison fight, by the way."

"So that fellow can't talk either. How convenient."

"If Clover nabs somebody and claims it's the shooter, don't be surprised."

"I'm half-expecting it."

ALI RETURNED HOME. After lunch with Scott, she'd gone to the office to address the troops. She was taking a few weeks off to bury her father and figure out what to do next. She fully intended to return, hopefully, with renewed vigor, because that was what her father, and especially her mother, would want. She put her number two, Megan Chambers, in charge and took her leave.

Now she opened the fridge for some chicken that had thawed overnight. She had promised Scott a home-cooked meal, but she couldn't deny the idea made her nervous. It was going to get difficult, for sure. She sprinkled a garlic-based seasoning on the chicken breasts and turned on the stove to warm the pan. While it heated up, she stood by the balcony window with a glass of wine. She was going to have a reaction when Stiletto walked through that door. She wasn't sure exactly what. Sadness because he wasn't her father? Guilt that she had broken off with him out of fear he'd be shot dead somewhere? Yet here he was, alive and well, and she had to bury her father.

Nothing made sense anymore.

WHEN STILETTO ENTERED THE CONDO, he found Ali at the stove. She said hello without turning around. He asked if he could help, but she had dinner mostly prepared. "There's beer in the fridge," she said.

Stiletto grabbed a bottle and sat at the counter. She flipped the chicken over. She'd assembled a salad, and two potatoes were baking in the oven.

She barely spoke to him, nor did she turn to look.

She served dinner at the table, and he told her

about his meeting with O'Brien. Ali had not known about Fairmont's mob connection.

"Why would he want my company? Just to launder money?"

"You ship all over the world and earn millions. He can launder money and smuggle stuff."

They ate quietly for a while, and Stiletto complimented the meal. The garlic gave the chicken a kick. His own efforts at cooking were only passable. He cooked a lot of chicken at home, but Ali did it right, keeping it moist, while his sometimes resembled toast.

"This isn't a simple police matter any longer, is it?" she stated more than asked.

"No. If we can get some proof and get it to O'Brien, we may have a chance at bringing Fairmont down."

"What about Clover?"

"I'm not sure about him." He mentioned the dead whistle-blower and Clover's arrest of the also-dead suspect. Ali made no comment.

They finished dinner and Ali poured coffee for herself, but stopped short of pouring a second mug. She made Stiletto a cup of tea, Earl Gray this time, which he gladly accepted, and they relocated to the deck. The cool air felt nice, and the traffic noise from the bridge seemed oddly soothing.

Stiletto unwrapped and cut a Macanudo Corona he had purchased on his way back. The wind carried the smoke away.

"We haven't had a chance to really catch up," she said. "Where are you living now?"

"Oh, you know."

"Same apartment?"

"Just bought a house." He laughed. "Then somebody broke in and shot up my car."

"What?"

"Related to another case, forget it. I have a neighbor who has three cats. She's older. Very nice. Another neighbor is a spooky Russian lady who talks on her porch all night, whispering in Russian."

"You should get a date with her."

"No, I like wondering if she's ex-KGB or something."

"Not much of a life, is it?"

He frowned at her. "What does that mean?"

She blinked, and he realized he'd spoken with a bit of an edge. He wanted to take the words back.

Too late.

"Don't get mad. I'm sympathizing. Jesus, I put

in so many hours that all I do at home is sleep. I don't have much of a life either."

She put her unfinished coffee on the little table between the chairs. "I'm going to bed."

Stiletto kept his mouth shut as she went back inside. She slid the patio door closed with authority. He finished his tea and smoked the cigar and admired the view some more, the bridge lights competing with the city lights across the bay. Things were going to be raw for them no matter what. He had to watch the attitude. She didn't need it, and neither did he if he was going to solve the problem. He felt angry about reacting the way he did. Should have known better. Why had he taken it the wrong way?

Because he was mad at her for leaving him. He sighed and shook his head.

When he was sure Ali was down for the night, he went inside to her little office nook just off the kitchen and turned on her computer. The monitor glowed brightly, and he switched on the desk lamp to reduce the glare.

He clicked on the Chrome browser and looked up Fairmont's company website.

FairSoft had a very efficient website, with sections for products, press releases, and investor relations. Scott clicked on the company's Dow listing, but the stock chart meant little to him. The graph seemed to show a downward trend, however. Articles confirmed that. Products had failed or been surpassed on the market, and the stock price had been falling steadily for some time, saved by the occasional uptick. FairSoft was no Apple. If Fairmont had a laundering arrangement with the Outfit, the condition of the company had to have strained the relationship. Such a strain might indeed drive a man to organize a murder to take over Ali's company.

Scott grabbed a beer and went back to the computer. Under About Us, he found pictures and bios of the company's top officers.

Martin Kent, CFO. Long résumé in the tech industry. Seemed clean enough.

Stiletto wondered what he was even looking for as he clicked the next name. The flare-up with Ali wasn't forgotten. Why was he mad? Sometimes relationships ended. Why wasn't that enough to quiet his mind?

He'd been in love with her, that was why.

He kept reading. Vic Williams was FairSoft's vice-president. Nondescript, and another corporate veteran.

Had she hurt him more than he wanted to admit? It was the only thing that made sense. Of course, she had. He hadn't wanted to end the relationship. He'd tried his best, and with time maybe he'd have overcome his issues, but it was all a moot point—and not the only reason she wanted out, anyway. Considering the circumstances, coming to her aid had not been a mistake, but it obviously wasn't the healthiest situation to enter into, and not because of Fairmont's thug, McCormick.

The next link highlighted Ben Pito, the corporate attorney. His bio mentioned past work in criminal defense and Stiletto's interest was piqued. He typed Pito's name into Google, and quite a history appeared. Articles about past cases defending syndicate goons in New York City and Chicago: a woman accused of drowning her son and various other baddies who, according to him, "deserved a good defense." It gave Stiletto an idea. He printed a picture of Pito and folded it into his wallet.

He turned in the chair to examine the quiet living room. No sounds from Ali's bedroom. The mess in the kitchen from dinner prep remained. He spent an hour doing the dishes and cleaning up, finishing with a wipe-down of the counter, and stood in the kitchen wondering what to do next.

BRIAN DRAKE

He couldn't abandon Ali. Being so high up in the tower meant it would not be an easy place to hit. The elevator ride up and the subsequent escape down would take too long even for a professional to make a clean getaway, but he still didn't like the idea of leaving. He found extra blankets in her father's bedroom and stretched out on the couch. She'd bought an expensive leather sofa, but the seats dipped like bucket seats in a car, and he shifted several times trying to get comfortable. He finally fell asleep after staring at the ceiling for a long time.

Sunlight blasting through the balcony windows woke him around six the next morning. He heard Ali splashing in the shower. Scott covered his eyes with a forearm and dozed off again until he smelled coffee, then sat up.

Scott wiped his eyes. The blanket had fallen on the floor.

Ali leaned against the kitchen counter holding a coffee mug. She sipped from it.

"You didn't have to stay," she told him.

"I don't think it hurt, just in case."

"You think—"

108

"Of course, now that I'm here. They can't hurt you, though. If they do, they lose. They'll try other things."

"I have to start making funeral arrangements," she said. "Should I bring my pistol? I have a Glock."

"Or I can go with you."

She drank some coffee.

He rose from the couch and approached, but a look from her stopped him halfway. "My apologies for last night," he said. "I don't know why—"

"Forget it," she said. "We're both as far out of our comfort zone as we can get."

"You shouldn't go out alone."

"And you slept in your clothes."

"Let's go to my hotel, and I'll change." He grabbed his wallet and keys from the coffee table.

"Have some tea first," she said.

STILETTO KEPT watch while Ali made her deals with the mortuary and cemetery. There were only rows of headstones, lingering visitors, and crews digging new graves. No sign of McCormick or any goons. With his arrival on the scene, they had to research *him* to see what kind of threat he might be. It did provide a bit of an advantage, but one that had to be taken right away. He unfolded the printed photo of Ben Pito and thought about his idea some more.

While Ali looked at a cemetery plot, Scott stood in the parking lot and called Toby O'Brien at the FBI.

"I think we should grab coffee again," Stiletto said.

"What's on your mind?"

"I want to know what you have on an associate of Fairmont's named Ben Pito."

"The lawyer?"

"He defended mobsters in New York. Maybe we can get something from him."

"I can't meet till evening. How about your hotel at eight tonight?"

"I'll bring Ali."

Stiletto ended the call and looked across the grounds, where Ali stood talking with the cemetery director. He did most of the talking. Eventually, they shook hands and went back inside the main building. A little later, she emerged with a folder under one arm. She didn't talk as they drove away.

Stiletto figured she had a right to know what he had in mind, but what to do after he told her was another story. She couldn't join him. It also might not be totally safe to leave her alone at the condo.

"Are you good with your pistol?" he asked.

"Sort of."

"We have a meeting with my FBI buddy tonight at eight, my hotel. After that, I'll be going out. Keep that gun handy."

"Do I want to know?"

Stiletto didn't fight his grin. "Anything I tell you makes you an accessory."

She didn't return the smile.

CHAPTER SEVEN_

Scott and Ali sat in a booth in Fast Eddie's Coffee Shop in the lobby of the Hyatt. A trio of men sat at the bar watching a TV mounted in the corner. The muted lighting and dark carpeting and walls provided more of a shadowy atmosphere than Stiletto would have liked.

Stiletto ate a BLT, but Ali refused anything but coffee. She was on her third cup of coffee, and Stiletto sipped water with lemon. He checked his watch.

"Should be here soon."

Ali did not reply. Her eyes remained on her coffee mug.

"Are you sorry you came?" she asked.

"What? No. Of course not."

"It can't be easy for you either."

"Because of us?"

"I didn't mean to hurt you," Ali said.

"Well, you did," he replied, "but the fact is I was hurting you too, and myself."

"Is it easier now?"

"Sometimes."

"Your daughter?"

"That remains unresolved. I don't know what to do."

She dropped her eyes to her coffee again. Stiletto didn't blame her. Nobody would know how to respond to that.

When Toby O'Brien entered, Stiletto felt a sense of relief. He wondered if Ali did too. Now they could direct their attention at him instead of each other, which was proving to be a bad idea.

The FBI man slid into the booth next to Ali, and they said hello and shook hands. Stiletto pulled out the printed picture of Ben Pito and handed it across the table as the waiter took O'Brien's order. O'Brien set the picture on the table and removed a notebook from inside his jacket.

"I had to dig into some old files to find out about this guy," O'Brien said. "He has indeed repped some wise guys in New York, but we have no definite connection between him and Califano. Except..."

"What?" Stiletto asked.

"He joined Fairmont's company about the same time Fairmont got cozy with Califano."

Ali inquired, "Who are you two talking about?"

Stiletto and O'Brien explained the suspected connection between Fairmont and the local mobster Califano. Ali shook her head.

"Max and the mob? I don't believe it."

"It's the only thing that explains what's happening," Stiletto said. "Where else do you think he found a thug like McCormick?"

"I found nothing on the big man, by the way," O'Brien said. "Covers his tracks well."

Ali shifted. "That's just crazy. Really? The mob is involved?"

"Fairmont's company is going south," Stiletto said. "Your company is not. He wants it so Califano doesn't have him killed."

O'Brien agreed. "If Fairmont goes under, the banks may discover the funny business. Can't have that."

"Wait," Ali said, "if it's the mob, that means

federal and that means FBI, which means you can take over, right?"

"We're only talking theory," O'Brien said. "Right now, I have no reason to get my people involved." To Scott, "Why Pito?"

"Maybe I can make him talk. If he's the connection between the two, his testimony can make the case."

"What are you suggesting?"

Stiletto shrugged. "A little persuasion."

"You want to go to prison?"

"I'm only planning on talking to him."

"So you'll lose your job instead?"

"Do you have another idea, Toby? If I can bring you a witness, you can start a case. Am I wrong?"

"This is dangerous."

"I only see you making excuses," Stiletto said.

"That's low."

"Scott," Ali exclaimed, "stop it."

Stiletto ignored her. "We're in the middle of a major criminal conspiracy that's claimed three lives that we know of. They're going to claim more. You can bet they'll try for me. Sitting on the sidelines isn't an option."

"If they want Ali's company so bad," O'Brien

said, "just wait them out. They'll get desperate and make a move, and then we'll have something."

"You may have Ali and me dead."

"There will be no support if you do this, Scott."

"Remember who you're talking to."

Ali frowned. "I don't like this."

Stiletto looked at her. "What else did you bring me out for?"

"I'm not sure anymore."

"There's no other way," Scott said. "Just let me try. If it doesn't work, we'll try the other way, as much as I think it's worse than what I have in mind."

"Just a conversation," O'Brien cautioned.

"You can bet Pito has something we can use against him."

Stiletto glanced at the two doubtful faces across from him.

Ali took a deep breath. "Okay."

"Toby?"

"I can't condone breaking the law."

"Cart before horse, Toby. I'm just going to talk to the guy."

"You and I both know it won't be that simple," the FBI man said. He reached into his jacket for a folded sheet of paper and passed it across the table.

"What is this?" Stiletto took the paper.

"Some notes you'll need."

Stiletto raised an eyebrow.

"I had to try to talk you out of it first," O'Brien told him.

SCOTT AND ALI inched through stop-and-go traffic on the way back to her condo. He drove one of her company's Lincoln Towncars.

"Traffic here is as bad as back home," he said.

"Uh-huh."

"Do you want me to go home, Ali?"

"You think that's all I'm thinking?"

"I'd very much like to know what you're thinking," he said.

"I thought I had left all this behind."

"What do you mean?"

"We dealt with murder, deception, backstabbing, shady deals, you name it, back at CIA. I wanted to get away from that, but it followed me here, and now you're going to continue the cycle. It's hard to process."

Stiletto sped up as the traffic flow increased. He made it through one intersection before a red light stopped him again. He kept looking forward because he felt Ali's eyes burning into him.

"Are you going to say anything?" she asked.

"What is there to say?" He glanced at her. "You're right. The sad part is, I don't know what else to do except be a hammer that pounds a nail."

"I don't know if my father would have wanted this."

"Would he want you to give up?"

"Maybe sell and find another way to beat Fairmont."

"With what resources?"

She sighed.

"You called me for a reason, Ali. Deep down you know why. You even said so in your note, so tell me again. Knowing what you know now, knowing that this wasn't random, what do you want me to do?"

The light turned green up ahead, but traffic didn't move.

Ali shut her eyes tight. Moments passed, and finally, she spoke.

"Kill them all."

. . .

Stiletto hadn't exactly come prepared for night combat.

The stores on Market Street hadn't closed yet, so he visited Macy's amidst the tourist crowd and purchased a pair of Timberland Gore-Tex hiking boots. From another store across the street, he bought a Stafford Topcoat that stopped just above his knees and offered adequate coverage for his shoulder holster.

He returned to the Hyatt and slung the Colt under his arm, covering the rig with the topcoat. The x-ray-proof bottom of his suitcase contained other tricks of the trade: a set of lock-picks, a pen flash, and a Buck pocket knife. The knife had a three-inch stainless blade with a razor edge. He stowed the items in the topcoat.

The boots fit well. A final check in the mirror showed no telltale signs of the gun rig, and Scott left the hotel.

As he rode the elevator down to the lobby, Stiletto knew he was stepping over the line—the line he had promised General Ike that he would not cross. Now that he was on the edge of that line, there was nothing to do but go all the way, because somebody had to stick up for those who couldn't defend themselves. Right now, that meant sticking up for Ali.

And that still counted, despite their differences.

He first visited the high-rise office building where Ben Pito worked.

Stiletto tried to enter the basement garage, but an electronic gate and a vigilant night guard dissuaded him. The guard stepped out of the shack.

"Can I help you?"

"Sorry, wrong turn."

The guard nodded, and Stiletto backed onto the street. He was on Main, and as he drove toward Howard, another car turned the corner, straddled both lanes, and stopped, blocking Stiletto's progress. Scott slowed, his right hand reaching for the gun under his left arm. Another car pulling the same trick appeared behind him.

Another try, guys?

Stiletto threw the Lincoln into reverse, stomping the gas, and the vehicle screamed toward the car behind him. The driver and passenger emerged with automatic weapons as he closed the gap. Stiletto aimed the rear bumper at the driver. The distance closed some more. The driver bolted for the sidewalk as Stiletto flashed by, the passenger pivoting to fire a burst that tapped the Lincoln's right fender but missed the tire. Stiletto swung around in a bootlegger turn.

The two enemy cars raced after him, their headlights bright in the rearview. A construction area occupied the corner lot on the other side of the intersection. Stiletto crashed the Lincoln through the security fence and slammed the brakes, skidding the car to a stop next to a portable building. He went EVA with the .45 in his right hand. The bright headlights of the other two cars shined on him as he moved for a concrete column. Automatic weapons fire crackled behind him, the shots splitting the air overhead. He made the column, rounds gouging the concrete and spitting chips into his face.

Stiletto dropped and leaned out as two of the gunmen converged. The other two, still in their vehicle, sped off to circle the lot and enter from another side.

Stiletto fired once, missing his intended target. The pair scattered. One dove for cover but didn't make it all the way, having to crawl the remaining distance. Stiletto fired twice. Both shots ripped through the man's back and pinned him to the ground. The gunman stopped moving.

The other returned fire in two quick bursts. Stiletto fired one shot in response and ran deeper into the construction area. Cement walls, scaffolding, pipes, and heavy equipment lay ahead.

The two shooters from the second car were making their way toward him from the opposite side of the site.

Footsteps scraped behind him.

Scott dropped into a crouch behind a lift. Part of the second floor was above him, making this the darkest part of the building. Street lights and passing cars cast moving shadows everywhere else. One of those shadows fired a test shot that went wide. Stiletto did not see the muzzle blast and he could not see the gunman, so he held his fire.

The echo of the shot faded. A chilly wind blew through the construction area and touched the back of Stiletto's neck.

Another footstep scraped concrete.

A piece of debris skittered across the ground.

A whisper.

Stiletto dropped onto his belly and crawled across the dusty concrete floor to a half-wall. Somebody shouted, "Now!" and a trio of muzzle flashes lit the darkened area.

Stiletto fired twice, shifted aim, and fired two more times. There was a scream, and the gunfire stopped. Whoever Stiletto had hit screamed again.

Scott reloaded the .45. A shot smacked the ground behind him, and he dived behind another wall.

Shadows drifted across the ground in front of him.

Movement on the left. Stiletto swung that way, lining up the .45 on a gunman's chest. The shooter raised his weapon as Stiletto's finger closed on the hair-trigger.

The Colt roared and kicked three times. The slugs ripped open the shooter's chest, and he fell into a puddle of his own guts.

Stiletto dropped and whirled to cover his backside. A flicker of movement to the right! He fired once. The last shooter scooted from his meager cover, letting off a string of covering fire. Scott hit the deck. He triggered another round that nicked the gunman's shoe.

Stiletto rolled left, sprang to his feet, and ran across a short open space to a wall. The last gunman tracked him and tore a chunk of concrete out of the wall as Scott reached it, but he stayed exposed too long. Stiletto caught him low in the belly with one shot, his follow-up tearing off the top of the gunman's head. The shooter's body hit the ground hard.

Stiletto ran back through the site to where he'd left the Lincoln. No sirens yet, but they'd come. He started the motor and powered out of there.

He steered straight for the Embarcadero and followed the road all the way to the Marina District near the Golden Gate Bridge. According to O'Brien's notes, that was where Ben Pito lived. His heart still raced and he kept his eyes peeled for anything out of the ordinary, but since he saw only normal traffic on the road, he decided he did not have any more shooters on his tail.

There had been no need to try to question any of the gunmen. He knew who had sent them, and to use a crew of that size indicated Fairmont and McCormick meant business. They wanted him dead *yesterday*.

He'd have to turn up the heat in return.

CHAPTER EIGHT_

STILETTO PARKED CURBSIDE a few doors down from Pito's house, and just in time, too. After a few minutes, the lawyer exited the two-story home and descended the steps to the white Audi in the driveway. He looked a little older than the photo on the website and news articles, had less hair, and was paunchier. The lawyer backed out of the driveway onto the street and Stiletto followed. With traffic as thick as it was once they reached Lombard, Scott had no trouble staying concealed and keeping the Audi in view.

They traveled down Lombard to make a right turn on Leavenworth, and after more stop-and-go, reached UN Plaza, where the lawyer parked and exited the car. With no other parking readily accessible, Stiletto drove by. He watched Pito stop in the center of the plaza near the statue of Bolivar on his horse, the equine rearing back with two hooves in the air.

The Civic Center/UN Plaza contained some of San Francisco's government and cultural institutions, concrete buildings creating a box around the plaza. Across the street, City Hall with its lit dome, the steeple on top of the dome scratching the night sky, oversaw the plaza.

Stiletto found parking in a small lot adjacent to City Hall. He raced across the street, weaving through the traffic and forcing some drivers to jam their brakes. The honking horns didn't get Pito's attention. As Stiletto slipped into an alcove on the side of one of the buildings, he saw the lawyer continue to look around the plaza, examining passing faces and checking his watch repeatedly.

The lawyer wore gray slacks and a white shirt with a tweed sports coat, hardly the kind of stepping-out clothes that blended with the other pedestrians or the homeless around the plaza. Maybe it was laundry day. Stiletto decided the man's wardrobe choices meant little in the grand scheme. Who was he waiting for? That was what Stiletto wanted to know.

A cold wind cut through the plaza and Stiletto shivered despite the heavy Stafford topcoat, which, he noticed, had a few nicks and tears from the gunfight. He shook his head. It was hard to keep nice things in one piece in his line of work.

Presently a man in a black leather coat with long black hair stepped up behind Pito, startling the lawyer, who let the man know he was displeased by the surprise. The man in the leather jacket held a briefcase, which he handed to the lawyer without comment. Stiletto heard Pito say this sort of thing wasn't even supposed to be part of his duties, but the other man didn't acknowledge the complaint. He turned and walked back the way he had come. Stiletto failed to catch a glimpse of the man's face since he'd managed to avoid any splash of light. Very good tradecraft, whoever he was.

Stiletto started across the plaza, heading for Pito's Audi, while the lawyer gathered his wits and started back toward the car on his own. Stiletto stopped to pretend to lace up his right boot, and when the lawyer drew abreast, he rose with the .45 in his right hand. He jammed the gun into Pito's belly.

"One word and I'll kill you."

Pito stared white-faced at Stiletto.

"Get in."

The lawyer fumbled for his keys, dropping them. He started to bend over, but a jab from Stiletto made him slow down. Carefully the lawyer retrieved the fallen keys and pressed a button on the fob to unlock the doors. As the lawyer slid behind the wheel, Stiletto climbed in the back and scooted to the passenger side.

The lawyer waited with his hands on the wheel.

"Where are you going?"

"To another place to hand over the case."

"What's in the case?"

"I don't know, I swear. This isn't my usual thing. They called me at the last minute."

"Drive."

Ben Pito fired up the motor and merged into traffic.

"I have to drop this briefcase by a certain time."

"You're gonna be late."

"My employers won't be happy."

"I may kill you," Stiletto told him, "so think about that."

The lawyer took a deep breath.

"I'm going to ask you some questions," Stiletto said. "Answer me honestly and I won't hurt you."

The lawyer laughed.

"Suddenly feeling confident?"

"What could you possibly want to ask me? I don't think you're representing any clients. I don't do criminal work anymore."

"Why does Fairmont want Ali Lewis's company?"

"Oh my God, you're—"

"You may know me as 'Mr. Hero.'"

When the lawyer stopped for a light, Stiletto spotted a freeway on-ramp ahead. He told Pito to get on the freeway.

"Well," Pito said. "Pleasure to meet you."

"Answer my question."

Pito drove across the intersection and veered left to join the 280 freeway.

"I don't know what Fairmont has in mind," Pito said. "I know his company is failing and he wants to stay in business. If he can't do it with software, maybe he can do it with fashion."

"Now it's my turn to laugh."

"He helped Ali's mother build that company. He's fully capable of running that kind of business."

"With Califano as a silent partner?"

"His deal with Mr. Califano is none of my business."

"Fairmont is responsible for a couple of murders, and for trying to have *me* killed," Stiletto said. "Tonight, in fact, before I intercepted you. Unfortunately, his guys are no good against somebody who knows his business. I don't think he's very good company for a lawyer who likes nice things."

"What does that mean?"

"It means I can promise you protection if you testify against your boss."

Pito laughed. "I wouldn't survive a day. You don't know half of what's going on here, do you?"

"Enlighten me."

"I'm not sure I even understand it all myself, but there are more people involved than just Fairmont and Califano," Pito said. "People from *overseas*, if you know what I mean. The kind we see on the news a lot."

Stiletto frowned.

"And if I'm going to be killed," the lawyer said, "I'd rather choose the way I go out. I could crash this car, you know."

"You might survive."

"You might not be so lucky."

"Ben, you're driving a new Audi. There are airbags all over. We'd both come out with a couple of scratches. You wouldn't accomplish anything."

Stiletto saw Pito's hand move toward his lap.

"Keep that hand where I can see it."

Pito nodded and put the hand back on the wheel.

The lawyer said, "I think we should test your theory." He stepped on the accelerator and the Audi surged forward. Stiletto's body pressed back into the seat. He licked his lips as the lawyer wove around other cars, increasing his speed from eighty to ninety to a hundred and ten. He held it there for a moment, then the needle climbed to a hundred and twenty.

The lawyer had to shout over the engine. "Never had it at this speed before!"

Pito continued dodging cars, moving at such a fast clip that the scenery blurred. The other cars were only flashes of light.

"Crash, already," Stiletto said.

Pito glanced at Stiletto in the rearview mirror. Stiletto saw the man smile.

. . .

PETER ROLLINS, Fairmont's golf buddy and business associate, sat in his office on the west side of the city. He was reading through the latest reports from his people on what he referred to as "the Project." The Iranians would be very happy. So far the numbers looked good, and he had no problems with the effort. When his phone rang, it disturbed the quiet room. Rollins frowned and answered, but nobody responded. What he did hear was voices in the background.

"Keep that hand where I can see it."

A voice he didn't recognize.

Then one he did. *"I think we should test your theory."*

Ben Pito.

Rollins heard a car engine growl. A few moments later Pito said, *"Never had it at this speed before!"*

The other voice: *"Crash, already."*

What the hell was going on?

He grabbed the phone on the corner of his desk, his landline, and quickly dialed.

"We have a problem," he told the person who answered. "I think Pito's been hijacked. He managed to dial his cell phone, and I'm listening to him and the other person in Pito's car. No idea where they are. Stay on the line, and I'll tell you what's going on. Yes, I *know* he has the case."

PITO SAID, "UH-OH" and let off the gas.

"Cold feet?"

"Cops."

Stiletto stashed his gun as Pito slowed the car and pulled to the side of the road. The blinking strobe flashed through the rear window and filled the car.

The officer leaned into the driver's side window.

"Somebody better be dying or I'm throwing you in jail," the highway patrolman began. His deep voice boomed.

Pito kept his hands on the wheel as the cop shined a bright flashlight into the vehicle.

"What's the story?"

"Got a little carried away, officer. We didn't mean any harm."

"Let me see your license and registration. It's not looking good for you unless I get a better story than that."

Pito didn't argue and produced the registration

and insurance paperwork from the glove box. The officer read the papers with his light.

"Mr. Pito," he said, "you know better than to do this. I have to impound the car. You know that."

"Officer, I assure you it was a momentary lapse in judgment, and it won't happen again."

The officer sighed and shined the light in the back seat.

"Why aren't you up front?" he asked.

Pito answered, "I was taking some friends home. He didn't feel like moving."

The officer put the light on Pito.

"I'll give you a warning this time, counselor, but not again." He handed back the papers.

"My word, officer."

The cop turned off his light and walked back to patrol car. As Pito returned the papers to the glove box, the cop sped by and merged back into the traffic.

"Friends in high places," Stiletto said.

"I do pro-bono work for the cops," Pito replied. "A lot of them know me. Gotta keep the bases covered." He started the Audi and drove off, then, "We're still in a stalemate, my friend. What would you suggest?"

"Take the next exit."

"Giving up?"

Stiletto laughed.

"I'll make you a deal," Pito said. "I'll let you out, and you walk away. I'll make up a story about why my delivery is late, and nobody has to know about this."

Pito steered the Audi off the Silver Avenue Exit and pulled over. Traffic flashed by.

"Now what?"

Stiletto leaned across the gap between them and bashed Pito in the head with the .45. The lawyer slumped in the seat unconscious, a wet red welt forming where the steel gun had hit. Stiletto exited the car, opened the passenger door, and tossed the briefcase into the back seat. He unbuckled Pito and dragged the lawyer's body to the passenger side. Taking the wheel, he hit the freeway again and made his way back to UN Plaza. He parked the Audi in a red zone. Pito didn't stir a bit. Exiting the car again, Stiletto took the brief-case, used the Buck knife to slash two of the tires, and returned to the Lincoln.

He found a parking ticket under one of the windshield wipers. He tossed that in the back and returned to Ali's condo. She answered on the first knock, and he slipped inside.

"Are you okay?" she said. "What happened?"

"Some rough stuff," he said. He removed the Stafford and his gun rig.

"Still carrying that Browning?"

"A .45 now," he corrected.

"What's in the case?"

"Let's find out."

They sat on the couch and placed the briefcase on the coffee table. Stiletto used his pick set to pop the locks and raised the lid.

"Light bulbs?" she said.

Stiletto took out one of the two items inside, both of which were nestled in foam containers. It indeed looked like a light bulb, albeit not of the usual shape. This one was longer, thinner, and rectangular. A sense of déjà vu hit Scott between the eyes.

"This is no light bulb," he said. "It's far worse. This is a krytron."

"A what?"

"A gas tube used to trigger a nuclear reaction inside a warhead."

Ali blanched.

"Whoa!"

"Now something Pito said makes a little more sense."

"What did he say?" Ali asked.

"That Fairmont has overseas partners of the kind we see in the news a lot. That job I did in Switzerland? It concerned Iranian agents trying to acquire a bunch of these."

"So you broke the Swiss connection, and they found one here in San Francisco?"

"Exactly. And I'll bet the farm this is why they want your company. Never mind the money laundering. They can move these around the world without a second glance from Customs people used to seeing your clothing shipments."

Ali sat back on the couch. "I have no words."

"I think it's time I got up close and personal with Mr. Max Fairmont."

He returned the krytron to the case.

"You have to tell General Ike," Ali said.

"Of course."

"What are you going to do with the briefcase?"

"I can keep it in the hotel safe for now," he said, "but that's not a good solution long-term. Keep your pistol handy, Ali. Things are going to start getting bloody."

"That's what I'm afraid of."

She leaned close to him, and by sheer reflex, he put an arm around her and pulled her closer. He felt her hot breath on his neck. "It's going to be okay."

"How many times can we say that without really believing it?"

"*I* believe it."

"I know you do." She lifted her head. "Kiss me."

He bent his head toward hers and their lips met, lightly at first, and then something happened. The kiss became deeper and more intense, their tongues meeting with a flash of pent-up desire that had finally found an outlet—residual embers catching fire.

He gently pushed her back on the couch.

WHEN PITO FINALLY CAME TO, he opened the passenger door of his Audi, leaned out, and vomited on the ground. A nearby homeless man sitting in a doorway said, "That's gross, man."

Pito coughed, wiped his mouth, and took note of his surroundings. His head throbbed where the gun barrel had struck, and he gingerly touched the stinging lump. He furiously patted his jacket pockets, looked around the floor in front, and found his cell phone. It had not been damaged. He dialed Rollins.

"Where are you?" Rollins said.

Pito explained the hijacking and said he'd lost the case. Checking the condition of his car, he noted the slashed tires. He told Rollins he'd need a ride and gave the man his location. Rollins promised to be there as soon as he could.

Pito stayed in his car and leaned back in the seat, his head still spinning. He wasn't aware of how much time ticked by, but eventually, another car pulled up beside him. He looked over as Rollins exited on the driver's side. The man who stepped out on the passenger side made Pito forget the pain in his head.

Rollins approached Pito, and the other man stood a little behind him. He had dark hair with blonde highlights. Pito knew he liked American jazz, and that his name was Shahram Hamin.

Rollins spoke. "Bad night?"

"I can't believe it, Rollins. He grabbed me after I made the exchange."

"Where's the case now?"

It wasn't Rollins who asked the question, but the other man, Hamin. Pito turned to him.

"I don't know."

Hamin took a deep breath and let it out slowly.

Rollins stepped back and conferred briefly with the Iranian agent.

"There was nothing I could do. He had a gun!" Pito insisted.

Rollins shook his head at Pito and returned to the car. Hamin stepped forward, removing a silenced pistol from under his coat. Pito screamed, and Hamin shot him in the face.

CHAPTER NINE_

I⟶ WAS GOING to be a long night.

Pito's information wasn't the only item listed in the notes provided by O'Brien. The G-man had also listed Fairmont's home address in Marin County.

As Stiletto drove the Lincoln across the Golden Gate Bridge, he thought about Ali. He could still feel the heat of her body on his skin. Was it easier now? Had enough time passed? The horrible thought that jumped into his head was that it would never be easier. He was fooling himself.

Stiletto drifted into the right lane to get around a slow truck and drove up the Waldo Grade and through the Robin Williams Tunnel, then took the Highway 1 turnoff prior to the Richardson Bay Bridge. He drove the winding Shoreline Highway until he came to Muir Beach. The curtain of night blacked out the surrounding scenery. His headlights carved a path through the darkness, and he found Pacific Way and drove to the top of the incline where Fairmont's home waited behind a gate, with a long driveway leading to the front doors.

He parked off the road and stepped into the wooded area surrounding the home. He found a low rise, dropped behind the foliage, and examined the grounds.

ADT Security signs had been placed strategically along the fence. Stiletto wasn't significantly deterred by those, but what did give him pause was the sight of an armed guard holding a dog on a leash. The guard carried a stubby submachine gun over one shoulder. The dog, a Doberman, wasn't to be taken lightly.

Stiletto watched the guard circle the grounds and, after about twenty minutes, walk out of sight. No other troops or animals appeared. That didn't mean there wasn't a team inside that rotated patrols.

Stiletto clenched a fist. He wasn't properly equipped and didn't want to charge headlong into a hot zone, but lights burned on the upper level of the house. Somebody—Fairmont—was home, and Stiletto had questions that required answers. He started formulating a strategy and checked his .45. He'd trade all the money he had for a silencer or a tranquilizer gun. There wasn't any other way to deal with the dog, but the shots would alert the entire house.

Sometimes, Stiletto thought, the job sucked.

Scott started hiking further along the fence to infiltrate closer to the house. When an engine revved and headlamps lit the grounds, Stiletto dropped flat.

A Jeep with two guards left a garage and traveled down the driveway to the main gate, where another car waited to enter. The Jeep stopped at the gate, one of the guards opened it, and the new arrival drove through. The pair in the Jeep escorted the car up the driveway to the house.

Two men exited the sedan, but the porch light wasn't bright enough to highlight their faces.

A late meeting, probably caused by the Pito interception. Good. Stiletto had rattled cages indeed. Now he really wanted to get in there and hear the pow-wow.

He rose and took a step toward the fence...

A twig snapped, and Scott spun around. Two figures in black rose from the brush. Before he could raise his gun, they had tackled and pinned him, and one used a stun gun to knock him cold.

ROLLINS KEPT to ten miles an hour as he followed the Jeep. Hamin occupied the passenger seat beside him. The Iranian had said nothing since disposing of the lawyer Pito.

Fairmont received them in his study, which was not only decorated with the usual bookcases and leather furniture, but with physical displays or photographs of the evolution of the personal computer.

It was all junk to Rollins.

Fairmont rose from a leather couch and offered them drinks. Rollins took a glass of Cutty Sark, but Hamin wanted nothing. The three men sat.

The Iranian spoke first. "Why am I only now learning about this problem you call 'Mr. Hero?'"

"Because we had it under control," Fairmont replied.

"Not the best choice of words, considering the loss of our items tonight."

"We sent four men to kill this person," Fairmont explained. "Rollins arranged it."

"I did indeed," Rollins agreed.

"How one man can get the best of four trained gunmen, I don't know," Fairmont said.

"He isn't some average Joe, as you say," Hamin said. "Did you check him out at all?"

"We did. We found his college information and military background, and then the trail went cold," Fairmont said.

"Nothing at all?"

"Zero."

"You're saying he's a ghost."

"If you want to say that, yes."

"And you have no idea what that may mean?" Hamin asked.

"Why don't you explain instead of hinting?" Fairmont told him.

"Easy, Max," Rollins said.

Hamin glared at Fairmont for a moment, then said: "It tells me that you should have told me in sooner. The only kind of person who would have a cold background would be a government operative, and I don't mean FBI. Do you have a picture?"

Fairmont nodded and took out his Samsung smartphone. He scrolled through the photos McCormick had previously sent. The shots showed Stiletto and Ali at lunch, the funeral home, and other places. Fairmont drew fingers across the screen to enlarge the best photo of Scott and handed the phone to Hamin.

The Iranian agent examined the picture with a growing frown. "I've seen this man up close."

"Who is he?"

Hamin returned the phone. "I do not know his name, but he is the reason I had to come here for my items. A similar arrangement I made in Switzerland was interrupted by this man and several associates, all of whom work for US spy agencies."

"You mean he's CIA or Homeland Security?" Fairmont asked.

Hamin shrugged. "Or another one."

Fairmont shifted in his seat, then bounced to his feet and started pacing. "What have we gotten into?"

Rollins remained steady. "Relax, Max."

"How? What we found out just now is that Ali has the kind of connections that can shut us down! If we kill him, they send more. When he was just another speed bump, it was no problem. Now it's a *huge* problem!"

"On top of your other issues," Rollins added.

"Don't remind me. I needed this deal. Badly."

"Here's the way I see it," Rollins said. He turned to face Hamin. "We have the ability to produce the items you require. What we're trying to get is the means to move them around the world with minimum risk. We thought the Lewis firm was the best choice, considering Max's earlier connection. If that's all we need, there are plenty of other companies we can approach."

Hamin did not reply.

"All it means is a loss of time," Rollins continued, "but we can make that up once we're squared away."

Hamin turned to Fairmont, who leaned with both hands on the back of his couch.

"We still have the FairSoft difficulties," Hamin said.

"My new product goes to the SalesForce show soon," Fairmont told him. "It's testing very well. It might buy us more time."

"We have a lot of loose ends," Hamin continued, looking at Rollins.

"Then we need to sew them up," Rollins said. "Tonight."

STILETTO WOKE up in the back of a van loaded with computer monitors. He wiped his eyes. The screens showed the Fairmont estate. Somebody sat in front of the monitors, but that wasn't the person Stiletto focused on.

Toby O'Brien sat beside him.

Stiletto said, "I think you have some explaining to do, pal."

"No kidding," the FBI man agreed. "Things got a little crazy just now."

"Why did you give me Fairmont's address only to have your guys sack me? Those stun guns *hurt*."

"You just crossed over into an active investigation," O'Brien said. "Without knowing it, of course. Heck, *I* didn't know it."

"I thought you had no business with Fairmont."

"We don't," said O'Brien. "We have business with one of the guys who showed up in the car. Does the name Peter J. Rollins ring a bell?"

"No." Stiletto sat up against the van wall. His side hurt a little, and he winced.

"Sorry about the taser," the man in front of the monitors said.

Stiletto ignored him. "Go on, Toby."

"Peter Rollins is an international go-between. He puts like-minded people who may not know of each other or have no way of getting in touch together for deals. We know he's been working with a man named Shahram Hamin for—"

Stiletto held up a hand. "I know. Now you've stepped on one of *my* investigations."

"Tell me."

Stiletto filled him in on as much as he could about Switzerland without saying too much.

O'Brien said, "So, Hamin needed a new connection for his nuke triggers. He found Rollins, Rollins found Fairmont, and here we are."

"You stopped me from going in there because now you can kill two birds with one stone," Stiletto mused.

"I suppose. We haven't thought that far ahead yet. I just needed you out of there."

Stiletto told him about the nuclear triggers he found in Pito's briefcase.

"Funny you mention that. Pito's body was found about an hour ago," O'Brien said. "Shot in the face. He's quite dead. But the killer didn't finish the job. A homeless person saw the whole thing and noted the license plate on the car the killer got back into. Rollins' car."

"There were two men in that car."

"Maybe Hamin was with him."

"Why haven't you moved on Rollins before now?" Stiletto asked.

"We don't know how they're getting the triggers, and now Fairmont's in the mix too. The only lead we have that may or may not even be connected is a missing scientist."

"Who?"

"A woman named Tina Avila went missing a few weeks ago, along with her son. She could be helping them, under duress or otherwise."

"Rollins doesn't have her?"

"We've followed him to a lot of places, but none that contain a potential hostage. His place isn't rigged with the kind of security needed to keep one, either."

"There were other things in Pito's briefcase," Stiletto said. "Maybe we can find a clue there."

"Where's the case?"

"Back at my hotel."

"Then that's where we go."

Stiletto took a deep breath and winced again. "I suppose I have to report to my boss."

"And vice versa. Maybe they'll let us pool resources."

"Where's my phone?"

O'Brien handed Stiletto his cell from a pile of his personal items. O'Brien handed back his gun, knife, lock picks and pen flash. Stiletto stowed the items and dialed Ali, but she didn't answer.

CHAPTER TEN_

ALI WATCHED television with very little comprehension. It was getting close to midnight, and she had heard nothing from Scott—just like the old days. Hours or days, or sometimes a month with no communication from him because of a mission. Her nerves couldn't take it, especially now.

The feelings honestly surprised her, but then she decided that nothing less could have occurred. Scott was part of her; part of her history. When their relationship had thrived, it had thrived indeed. One can move on, but can never erase history. Their little encounter on the couch upon which she sat might have simply been a release of tension, nothing more. She couldn't keep her thoughts straight, and they bounced around her head like pinballs.

She had not ignored his departing piece of advice. Not only did her Glock-17 automatic and a spare magazine sit on the coffee table, but she had put on Levis and a black t-shirt and running shoes. She'd sleep in the outfit if she had to, just in case. Car keys, driver's license, and a money clip were in the pockets of the jeans.

She wasn't an expert shot or a combat vet, but everybody who joined the CIA had to visit the Farm and learn the basics. She knew how to shoot at a respectable level, but it was all theory, shored up with a little practice a dozen years ago, and very little since. How she'd fare under pressure was another story. She'd never fired at anything other than paper targets, or moving objects that didn't fire back. And then something crashed into the door. A heavy thud. Wood cracked. She snapped out of her trance, snatching the gun as she moved for the cover of her corner dining table.

The door frame had bent inward, the wood splintering. Another thud and the whole door crashed open, three men framed in the doorway as they entered. One tossed aside a battering ram.

McCormick was in the lead, toting an ugly black Uzi.

She pointed the Glock at him and fired three times. Each shot missed as he dashed right at her and shoulder-rolled onto the carpet. The second man broke left for the kitchen. She fired once at him and missed. The third man let off some covering fire as he entered the room, but he didn't move fast enough. Ali's next two rounds impacted with a *whack-splat* that sent a spray of blood and tissue into the hallway behind him. His body fell in the doorway.

Smoke trickled from the muzzle of her pistol. Seventeen rounds in the mag to start, but how many had she fired? Her spare mag still sat on the coffee table. It might as well have been one hundred miles away.

The shooter in the kitchen fired and she shot back, then swung her sights to McCormick, who jumped up and ran for her bedroom. Her two shots shredded the doorway as his body dived through.

The kitchen gunner rose, and she fired once to keep him down. She had to get her spare ammo. She fired once at the kitchen and once at the bedroom wall and left the dining table, rushing on hands and knees to the coffee table. McCormick leaned out of the bedroom, and the flash from the Uzi filled the room. Ali dropped flat on the carpet between the two tables. The large windows behind her shattered and huge pieces of glass flew inside in the sudden rush of wind. She covered her neck. Pieces landed on her and around. She raised her gun and fired four rapid shots. No idea where they landed, but McCormick moved back.

She lunged forward, reaching for the spare magazine. The kitchen gunner blasted the table in half, the mag falling to the floor. She fired once, twice—and the Glock locked open, empty. She scrambled into the space between the couch and wrecked table as the kitchen shooter rose again. She flung a loose table leg at him and he ducked, the leg crashing into the stove. She ejected the empty magazine, grabbed the spare, and reloaded, closing the action as she rose to full height. The gunman in the kitchen swung his gun on her for the last time. Her single shot sprouted for him a third eye that grew between the other two, blood and bone fragments blasting out the back of his head to splatter the white kitchen tile.

McCormick stepped out again, the Uzi at his hip. As Ali leaped onto the couch and stepped onto the back, launching herself into the air, his burst turned the couch into rubbish, shredding the cush-ions. Stuffing flew everywhere as Ali landed, executing a textbook tuck-and-roll across the carpet.

She stopped at the dead body in the doorway. Firing back at McCormick, she forced him to hide long enough to grab the dead man's Uzi. Gripping the submachine gun in both hands, she sprayed the bedroom doorway and the adjacent wall. The high-velocity slugs ripped through as if the wall were paper. McCormick didn't scream, but something had to have hit him. *Had to.*

The Uzi clicked empty. She dropped it and grabbed the dead man's pistol and spare ammo pouch, then she ran, crashing through the stairwell door and pounding down the staircase as fast as she could. The beating pulse in her head was the only thing she could hear.

She wasn't supposed to have a gun!

As McCormick dove through the bedroom doorway, he heard Ali's second or third salvo hit behind him. She wasn't very good with the gun, for sure, but she had one, and his simple snatch-and-grab had just gone ka-blooey. He hadn't had any second thoughts about this job until now. She wasn't some sucker. She had Mr. Hero and her own gun. Max had said he knew the Lewis family well, but apparently, not as well as he thought.

By the time she grabbed the other Uzi, he knew he was over his head. She shouldn't have known how to use that. He dived behind her bed as the burst sliced through the wall. She was smart enough to know she might hit him that way. He was smart enough to figure she'd try.

When the Uzi went silent, he cautiously stepped through the doorway. Gone. Stuffing from the couch still hung in the air.

With his two guys dead, he wasn't going back to Max empty-handed. His orders had been explicit—take her alive to lure Mr. Hero into a trap, then kill them both.

As McCormick reloaded and ran after her, he grabbed his phone and called for backup. He didn't tell them the silly bitch had just made a fool out of him. She was going to pay for that.

Ali stopped, breathless, before the door to the lobby. She couldn't go charging through with two semi-auto pistols. She jammed the guns into her waistband and covered them with her t-shirt.

She pushed through the lobby door, crossing the marble tile to the garage door opposite. The desk where the security guard normally sat was empty, and sirens wailed in the distance.

She didn't want to take a chance with the cops. If Inspector Clover was in league with Fairmont, other cops might be too.

She entered the quiet garage and dug for her keys. Racing to her BMW, she tossed the guns on the passenger seat and dropped behind the wheel. Sweat dripped into her eyes and she dashed it away, using her other hand to wipe her face. Her lungs burned from the rush down the stairs, but so far she was still alive.

The engine roared to life, and the tires squealed in reverse. She powered forward, following a curve to the exit and increasing her speed as the BMW drew closer to the opening.

Another car bumped the curb as it swung into the garage, and when it jerked to a stop with two men piling out, Ali slammed the brakes. Both men held automatic weapons. She dived for the floor as they opened up on the car, the BMW rocking with the impacts. The windshield sprouted a dozen spider-cracks but did not break.

Ali pushed open the passenger door and rolled out with a pistol in either hand. She returned fire, the guns kicking back, and the shots found their marks. The shooters twitched and fell, their guns clattering beside them.

The Glock was empty again, so she left it there and reloaded the stolen gun—a Beretta.

She ran out into the dark street. The cool air felt good on her sweaty skin. To her left was the front of the building. Behind her was a path to the Embarcadero with plenty of alleys and doorways offering a place to hide. The sirens grew louder, and police cars swarmed the front. She turned to run the other way. Another cop car careened around the corner ahead, and the bright headlamps shined on her and the gun she clutched. The police car screeched to a halt, and two officers jumped out with drawn guns.

"Drop it! Get on the ground!"

Ali didn't argue. She tossed away the pistol and stepped away with her hands up.

"On the ground!"

She dropped to her knees first, then stretched out flat.

One of the cops approached, kicked away the Beretta, and holstered his weapon. Removing his handcuffs, he grabbed Ali's left wrist and...

"Watch it, Harry!"

The cop who remained by the car shouted the warning way too late.

McCormick emerged from the exit and raised the Uzi. His first burst cut down the cop who had spoken. The officer by Ali went for his gun, only to have the next burst of nine-millimeter high-velocity stingers cut through his neck and head.

Ali screamed, rising to grab the Beretta. She heard other yells behind her, but more chatter from the Uzi drowned them out. She dived for the gun, wrapped her fingers around the plastic grips, and started to turn. The image of her dead father flashed in her mind as she raised the gun on McCormick.

The long trigger pull on the Beretta kept her from getting off a fast shot, and McCormick was on her. He lashed out with a kick that sent the gun flying from her fingers and pain flashed through her hand.

She started to scream again, but McCormick swung the Uzi's metal butt-stock against her head and turned out the lights.

．．．

STILETTO TRIED Ali's phone again and cursed when she didn't pick up.

It was his fourth call since leaving Fairmont's place.

O'Brien finally turned onto the Embarcadero. The drive was taking too long as far as Scott was concerned, but O'Brien had the speedometer hovering just over the limit, so it wasn't a case of driving slow.

"We're almost there," O'Brien said.

ALI FELT cold water on her face.

She awakened very slowly, feeling more pain then she had ever experienced. The left side of her face throbbed, and she rolled over and retched. The white-tiled floor was also cold. The walls were white as well, and the fluorescent lights above only accentuated the flat color.

"How badly are you hurt?"

The voice came from the person holding the cold washcloth. A woman with long dark hair, olive skin, and dark eyes.

"They brought you here a few minutes ago," the woman told Ali.

"Who are you?"

"I'm Tina Avila. They've kept me here for weeks, maybe longer. They have my son, too."

O'BRIEN ROLLED up on the scene in front of Ali's building—cops, several ambulances, and general chaos. A lot of flashing cherry lights.

A uniformed patrolman waved them on. O'Brien steered away and took the next right.

"Go back and show them your badge," Stiletto said. "We need to get in there."

"And get us into a territory dispute with the supervising officer? Not worth it. We'll never get through that perimeter."

"Toby—"

"Scott, now's the time to call headquarters. Both of us. Ali will have to go it alone until we can get to her."

Stiletto wanted to argue further, but Toby was right. He had to update the general.

CHAPTER ELEVEN_

ALI ASKED, "WHERE ARE WE?"

"I'm not sure," the other woman said. "Sometimes I hear loud music above the ceiling."

Ali rose to her hands and knees, then braced herself on a cluttered table to get to her feet. The items on the table gave her pause. Glass tubes. Filaments. Electronic circuits.

"Nuclear triggers," Ali stated.

"How do you know?" Tina Avila asked, stopping beside Ali.

"I've seen your work already. You a physicist?"

"Yes. Who are you?"

Ali gave Tina a condensed version of events.

Tina grabbed Ali's arms tight. "Your friends have to stop! The Iranians have my son."

Ali shoved her away. "Unless you have a phone, I can't very well warn them."

Tina Avila put a hand to her mouth and backed away.

"How many krytrons are you making? Tell me, Tina. How many?"

The other woman lowered her hand. "They want a thousand. I've made maybe two hundred."

"Where do you keep them?"

"They're gone. Two men come to collect them now and then."

The door on the other side of the room opened and McCormick entered.

"You're coming with me," he said, grabbing Ali by her left wrist. He started to drag her toward the door. Ali kicked him, and he turned and smacked her. As her head snapped to one side, he scooped her up and over his shoulders.

McCormick carried Ali down a short concrete hallway to another room, placed her in a chair, and tied her wrists behind the back and her ankles to the legs. He slapped her awake, and she raised her head. A single light burned above her, and the concrete walls were bare. She noted boxes labeled with the names of various brands of alcohol stacked in corners.

"Where am I?"

"I ask the questions, honey."

"Go to—"

He slapped her hard. Her face stung.

"Where is he?" McCormick asked.

"Santa Claus?"

He slapped her again in the same place. She groaned.

"Mr. Hero. Your boyfriend."

"Ex," she corrected.

He leaned close to look into her eyes. He smelled musty.

"You're not funny."

"I'm going to kill you, McCormick."

"I won't be as easy to kill as your old man was."

A red flush crawled up her neck and she strained hard against the bindings, but they didn't budge. McCormick folded his arms and smiled. Ali spat in his face.

He removed a handkerchief from his coat pocket and wiped his face.

"You couldn't just take the money?"

"It's never been about the money."

"Where is he?" McCormick stepped closer.

"He'll get here soon enough," she assured him.

He smacked her again. Third time in the same spot. She didn't feel the sting any longer.

"Having fun?"

"What is it about you?"

"Tell you what," Ali said. The right side of her face was red, matching the color of the welt from being hit by the Uzi. She breathed hard. "Just so you know. I'm a former CIA officer, and my ex? He kills people for a living. People like you."

McCormick froze in place, then turned for the door. He left her there.

"Obviously," General Ike Fleming said, "the situation has evolved."

"You have a talent for understatement, sir."

"Are you still with O'Brien?"

"He's outside the car on the phone with his boss."

"You can't take an active role, Scott, but I can give you a temporary transfer to the Domestic Protection Division, which will allow you to consult."

"So the FBI gets Hamin?"

"Once he's in the system, we'll take over like we have a hundred times before."

"Okay," Stiletto agreed.

"Do you have any idea where to look for Ali?"

"None."

"Better get cracking and find one. Oh, and Scott?"

"Yes, sir?"

"Please be careful not to miss any sudden opportunities."

"I'll do my best to create them."

"Good luck."

"Thank you, sir."

STILETTO PUT his phone away as O'Brien returned to the car. "What did he say?"

"I'm allowed to consult."

"Good. My boss is up to date, and we got a warrant for Pito's home and office."

"Let's hit the office. The good stuff will be there."

O'Brien started the car.

THE DASH CLOCK read nearly two a.m., and as they drove across town, Stiletto and O'Brien passed several bars and clubs that were depositing their drunken clientele on the street. They eased through the more congested spots without incident.

A squad of FBI with an accompanying evidence crew awaited O'Brien at Pito's Main Street office. Building Security let them in and told the agents their colleagues were already upstairs. O'Brien and Scott exchanged a look.

O'Brien ordered the squad and evidence team to stay in the lobby. He and Scott rode the elevator to the twentieth floor.

"Where'd they get the credentials?" Stiletto asked.

"Probably off the Internet," O'Brien said. "Very few see a genuine FBI badge, so fakes are easy to get away with."

The elevator stopped at the twentieth floor. O'Brien and Scott stepped into the lobby and went down a hallway to the stairs, taking out their pistols as they carefully climbed to the twenty-first floor where Pito had his office. They moved sideways, backs to the wall, O'Brien looking up and ahead while Stiletto watched the space behind them. Neither spoke. Some cigarette butts lined the steps, and graffiti decorated the walls. At the door to the twenty-first floor, they stopped. Stiletto opened the door enough to peek through with one eye. He shut the door.

"One man by the elevator," he reported. "In a suit."

"They thought of everything." O'Brien traded his gun for an ASP Expandable Baton. He flicked his wrist, and the metal baton snapped to its full length of twenty-one inches. O'Brien had put a small smiley face sticker on the grip.

"Nice touch," Stiletto said.

Stiletto opened the door, and O'Brien charged through. Scott followed him, the Colt .45 in his right hand.

The guard opened his mouth to shout an alarm, but O'Brien swung the baton before any sound escaped the man's lungs. It struck the side of the man's head with a hollow *thwack*, and Stiletto caught the guard and lowered him to the floor. O'Brien put away the ASP and took out his gun once more.

Ceiling lights flickered as they advanced down the hallway. Presently they came to a set of double doors with a sign that read Pito Legal Services. The right-side door was already open a few inches, but no lights burned in the office.

The hinges did not squeal as O'Brien led the way through the doorway.

Past the reception desk was a bullpen of cubicles. Beyond that was Pito's corner office, with two windows looking out on the city.

Two more thugs in suits were stuffing a tote bag without paying attention to the door.

Stiletto put the glowing sights of the .45 on the thug behind the desk while O'Brien covered the other.

"FBI! Freeze!"

The two men turned to look at them in what seemed like slow motion. One of them blinked in surprise.

"Let's see those hands! Raise 'em!"

The one behind the desk brought up his right hand, which held a pistol. Stiletto's index finger barely twitched, and the .45 slug punched through the man's head and cracked the window behind him.

The second thug lifted both hands above his head. "Don't shoot! I give up!"

O'Brien ordered the man out of the office and against the wall. Stiletto kept the man covered while O'Brien patted him down. He removed a wallet, cell, and car keys from the thug's pockets.

After snapping cuffs on the man's wrists, O'Brien sat him in a chair.

"What's the rumpus?" O'Brien said. "You ain't washing windows."

The thug, breathing hard, stared at the carpet.

"We got you red-handed raiding the office of a man who has just been murdered," O'Brien said. "You're going away for a long time unless you help us."

The thug shook his head.

Stiletto remarked, "You feel that?"

"Feel what?" O'Brien asked.

"There's a draft from that crack in the window. Wouldn't be hard to make it larger by throwing this guy through."

"You've seen too many movies."

"Telling us a thing or two beats taking a flying lesson without an airplane."

"Well," O'Brien said, "I suppose we could see how big a splat he makes."

Stiletto and O'Brien grabbed one of the thug's arms and started to pull him out of the chair. He struggled, yelled, and finally said, "Okay!"

"Okay, what?"

"The boss told us to come in here and take everything."

They dropped him back in the chair.

"Who's the boss?"

"Califano."

"How perfect is that, Scott?"

"Let's see the goods," Scott demanded. He and O'Brien went into the office to sort through the totes.

They dug through the papers and notebooks. O'Brien found a flip-up notebook with a bunch of words crossed out and set it aside. The papers all contained lawyer stuff. It wasn't until Scott found a USB thumb drive at the bottom of one of the totes that they stopped searching.

Stiletto plugged the USB into his smartphone via an attachment provided by O'Brien. It opened a window of file folders. Stiletto tapped one, but it asked for a password.

"Guys at the office can crack this," O'Brien told him.

"We don't have that kind of time."

O'Brien picked up the flip-up notebook again. "Try this." He pointed to the word at the bottom of the list that was not crossed out and Stiletto entered the word Engine. The password prompt vanished and the folder Stiletto had tapped opened.

Stiletto opened a file called FAIRMONT1.

He scrolled through several files and opened FAIRMONT2 and FAIRMONT3. O'Brien read over his shoulder.

"Eureka," Stiletto exclaimed.

O'Brien called the team in the lobby. "We're secure. One dead, one in custody. Send everybody up."

WHILE THE EVIDENCE team loaded boxes of material from Pito's office, Stiletto and O'Brien sat in the FBI agent's car and read through more of the USB files.

It was indeed the proverbial mother lode. Pito kept detailed records on every aspect of Fairmont's operation, ranging from his first meeting with Califano to his most recent meeting with Peter Rollins. It also included information on the kidnapping of a physicist named Tina Avila to assemble krytrons for the Iranians.

Detailed notes included how best to take over Ali's company.

There were notes on the locations the Iranians frequented and where Tina Avila was being held, along with the location of her son, whom they were holding as leverage to make her do their dirty work.

Not included in the notes was information on the murder of Ali's father.

Lars Blaser had been right.

They found somebody else.

"We can bust them wide open with this," O'Brien stated.

"Maybe they're holding Ali in the same place as Avila? Says here, Club Fugazi."

"That's a Califano club."

"We should get her kid first," Scott said. He highlighted the address and showed it to O'Brien.

"Know this place?"

"Out near Ocean Beach. Other end of the city. Bit of a drive."

"I suggest we get started."

O'BRIEN GASSED up at a corner Shell and turned onto Market, and presently made turns onto Turk and Arguello and eventually Fulton, which, he said, went all the way to Ocean Beach. With the magnetic red cherry light on the roof, O'Brien stayed above the speed limit. They hit mostly green lights on Fulton, but he went through the reds after slowing to check each intersection.

He made a right turn onto the Great Highway, and presently pulled over a block away from a single-level home built on the slope of a hill. Waves crashed off to their left, but the ocean and sand, totally dark, resembled an abyss.

"It's a Califano safe house," O'Brien said.

"The Godfather is turning up everywhere," Stiletto said. "We're a little light on hardware, though."

O'Brien grinned and pressed a button under the dash to pop the trunk. Stiletto followed him out.

The air was tinged with salt, and the wind carried the ocean mist. Scott felt the moisture settle on his face and neck.

O'Brien lifted the trunk. Secured under the lid were an M-4 carbine and a Remington 870 pump shotgun. O'Brien unzipped a tote containing ammunition for both. Flak vests sat on the trunk floor. O'Brien handed Scott one.

"You're probably better with the M-4 than me," O'Brien said as he tightened the Velcro straps of the vest. "You can take that one. It's full-auto."

Stiletto removed his topcoat, put on the vest, replaced the coat and took the M-4 from its clamps. He opened the action and felt inside with a pinky finger. A layer of oil coated the action. He grabbed three fully-loaded magazines from the tote. Two went into pockets, and the third he locked into the M-4.

O'Brien fed rounds into the 870 and stuffed spare shells into his own pockets. He pumped the 870 and flipped on the safety.

"Ready?"

Stiletto nodded.

O'Brien gently closed the trunk, and the two men started up the road to the house. Scott's heart rate increased as they neared.

It wasn't the best way to hit the place, but time was running out and they had no choice. If Fairmont was making overt moves against Ali now, who knew what he was going to do next? They also had no idea how many opponents they faced. The Avila boy could have been moved as well, which meant the house might even be empty. No lights burned inside, but even mafia thugs needed sleep. Stiletto stepped onto the empty driveway first, then O'Brien, and then the spotlight hit them.

The light blazed from an open window, and they hit the ground as pistol shots cracked. The rounds whined overhead as Stiletto let off a three-round burst. Glass shattered, a man screamed, and the light went out.

O'Brien jumped up and ran toward the door, firing the shotgun twice. He kicked open the door, entered, and rolled left. Stiletto, on his heels, swept the M-4 from right to left.

They were in the front room, which contained couches, chairs, and a piano. There was a hallway straight ahead. A gunman near the piano rose with a pistol, and Stiletto pinned him to the wall with another burst. The gunman tumbled back into the wall, fell, and got tangled in some curtains, leaving a trail of red as he hit the ground.

"FBI, give up!"

Another gunman fired twice from a doorway along the hall. Scott fired back, only to miss and tear chunks out of the wall.

The gunman emerged again, this time to pitch a smoke grenade their way. The living room filled with smoke, which stung Stiletto's eyes and went up his nose. He coughed, dropping low. Somewhere, a boy screamed.

Stiletto ran into the smoke, only to collide with the hallway gunner. He might as well have tried plowing through a brick wall. He saw enough of the man to know he was not only huge but wore a gas mask. The collision had sent the man's gun flying, but he was still ready for a fight.

He slammed Stiletto against the wall and Scott exhaled sharply. The gunner tried to wrench the M-4 from Scott's grasp, but he held tight, pulling the gunman closer. He jerked up a knee to hit the thug between the legs but missed. The gunman kept one hand on the M-4 and grabbed a fistful of Scott's shirt with the other. He kicked one of Stiletto's legs out from under him and shoved the agent to the floor, landing on top, then grabbed Scott's neck and squeezed.

Scott choked, gagging, his eyes still hot and wet from the smoke. He heard the 870 boom from somewhere in the house.

The breeze from the open front door began clearing some of the smoke. Through the plastic visor of the gas mask, Stiletto watched the gunman's unblinking eyes go wide as he squeezed harder.

Stiletto let go of the M-4 and grasped the gas mask, yanking it aside, exposing one eye and obscuring the other.

The remaining smoke hit the gunman hard. His one big eye took the brunt of it and he recoiled, clamping a hand over the eye. He tried to adjust the mask but Stiletto pressed the index and middle finger of his right hand together, then blasted a two-finger strike into the gunman's throat.

The gunman let out a squeal and jerked away, and Scott rolled to his knees. The gunman tossed the mask and started to charge again.

The Buck knife snapped open in Scott's hand and he met the gunman halfway, plunging the knife into him. The blade tore through his clothing to rip deep into his flesh and blood spilled onto Stiletto's hand. The gunman screamed in Scott's ear. Scott stabbed him again and again, and the thug's dead weight fell against him. He shoved the gunman away, wiped the bloody knife on the man's pants, stowed it, and picked up the M-4.

Residual smoke from the grenade hung in the air. Scott leaned against the wall for a moment.

An engine roared, and something crashed outside.

Stiletto shoved away from the wall and ran deeper into the house.

TOBY O'BRIEN SHUT his eyes and clamped his free left hand over his nose and mouth as the room filled with smoke. The last thing he saw before the smoke engulfed the room was the doorway to the kitchen—straight ahead, past the piano and corner dining table.

He ran that way, catching a foot on the leg of a chair. He fell face-first onto the carpet. A boy screamed from the kitchen, and O'Brien jumped up and ran through the doorway.

A fourth gunman hauled a ten-year-old boy from the laundry room adjacent to the kitchen. The man kept the boy close, but the boy twisted out of the man's grip, and for a split second O'Brien had a kill shot. As he tightened on the 870's trigger, the gunman pulled the boy to him again. O'Brien raised the muzzle at the last instant.

The gunman pulled the boy across the tiled floor to a patio door.

The gunman fired at O'Brien and opened the door, dragging the boy outside. O'Brien started to follow but the gunman fired into the house, the Fed hitting the floor as stingers shredded the cupboard and refrigerator to his right.

O'Brien jumped up and ran outside in time to see the thug carry the boy around the corner.

O'Brien stopped at the corner and peeked around. A shot from the gunman hit the outer wall and spat bits of shrapnel into O'Brien's face. He yelled, ducking back. A doorway to the garage was midway down the path, and O'Brien heard the door rumble open. He turned the corner and advanced.

A motor started.

O'Brien ran.

As he cleared the doorway, the black SUV plowed backward through the garage door, whole pieces clinging to the back of the vehicle.

O'Brien fired once, pumped the action, and fired again, the Magnum loads hammering the wooden stock into his shoulder. The SUV sank sideways, the front and rear passenger-side tires now flat with the vehicle half out of the garage. O'Brien pumped again and took aim. His next blast shattered the windscreen and took off part of the gunman's head. The SUV idled in reverse, the steel rims of the flat tires screeching on the concrete.

O'Brien ran to the driver's side and yanked open the door. He reached across the dead gunman, engaged the emergency brake, and looked at the frightened boy on the floor of the passenger side.

The boy pointed over O'Brien's shoulder.

"Look out!"

O'Brien waited for bullets to tear into him as he spun around.

"Hey!" Stiletto shouted, raising the M-4 over his head.

O'Brien lowered the shotgun.

Police arrived first to secure the scene and kept Scott and O'Brien apart while they waited for an FBI supervisor. Once they were cleared, the supervisor told them to get the Avila boy to the hospital. They waited outside the examining room while a nurse checked the boy, and Stiletto paced anxiously.

"We can't stay here," he insisted.

O'Brien handed him the keys to the car. "Don't get caught."

CHAPTER TWELVE_

THE NUMBERS WERE FALLING FAST NOW.

Stiletto punched the Club Fugazi address into the FBI vehicle's GPS and followed the voice commands to the address on Green Street. He circled the block a few times. It was well past four a.m. now, so the streets were virtually empty, as were parking spaces near the club. The neon lights out front still blazed and cast a colorful glow across the street. Nobody on the street seemed part of any elaborate security display. He made one final orbit, noting the side alley and back exit and the three cars clustered near it.

Stiletto drove around the front once more and parked near the entrance. A doorman was sliding a chain lock through the handles of the front door, and he ignored Scott. Then he saw the shotgun and put up his hands. Stiletto clubbed him with the butt-stock, dragged the unconscious man out of the way, pulled the chain out, and pushed inside.

The place was well-lighted, spotless...and empty. Bar stools were stacked, dining chairs had been placed on tables, and all debris associated with a night of revelry cleared from the dance floor. A staircase on his right led to a private office, where he heard voices even though the door was closed. Stiletto kept the shotgun beside his leg. At the top of the steps, he kicked the door open, and it slammed against the opposite wall. Stiletto went in with the shotgun at his hip and pointed the muzzle at a man seated behind the desk in front of him.

The man didn't seem surprised.

The other man in the room, McCormick, went for a gun but froze when the man at the desk snapped his fingers.

"Speak of the devil," the man said. He was pushing seventy, large and rotund, nose bent, age spots dotting his face. "The ex-boyfriend. Super-assassin."

"Mr. Califano, I presume," Stiletto said. "Where's Ali?"

McCormick grinned. "Nowhere you'll ever find her, Mr. Hero."

Stiletto stiffened as the cold snout of a gun touched the back of his neck.

Califano said, "Just in time, Inspector Clover."

McCormick came forward and jerked the shotgun out of Stiletto's grasp. He handed it to Clover, who put away his pistol and jammed the 870 into Scott's back.

McCormick searched Stiletto and collected the Colt and the Buck knife. He stepped back.

Califano said, "Your lady says you're some kind of hotshot secret agent. I think she said that to put a scare into us, and she spooked McCormick. Right, McCormick? Heh-heh. I think you're funny. Barging in here, only to get stuck up by a beat cop. Hey, Clover?"

"Yes, sir."

"Take this garbage out of here."

Clover, prodding with the shotgun, forced Stiletto back down the stairs and outside.

Stiletto stopped on the sidewalk.

"Now what?"

"Turn left. Down the alley."

Stiletto's hiking boots scraped the pavement as he followed directions. The alley was dark, with only a slight spillover from the street lamps illuminating the space. It was enough. Part of a broken pallet stuck up out of a dumpster.

Stiletto spun, dropping low and slamming a fist into Clover's solar plexus. As the cop cried out and doubled over, Stiletto pulled the board from the trash and smashed it over the inspector's head. The board split on impact but the cop dropped flat, unconscious.

Stiletto picked up the shotgun. He reentered the club and climbed the steps to Califano's office.

The Outfit boss sat alone, lighting a cigar. He stopped mid-puff, incredulous at the sight of the man in the doorway.

"Still laughing?"

Stiletto fired once and the blast opened Califano's chest and neck, blood and torn flesh splattering the desk and carpet. Califano's body tipped forward, and his face landed on the desk with a thud.

No McCormick. Where was he?

Stiletto hustled to the dance floor, looking around frantically for a clue. Pito's notes had said the club was where they'd stashed the physicist, Tina Avila. Had they stashed Ali here too?

A door across the floor said AUTHORIZED

Personnel Only. Stiletto ran to it, yanked it open, and followed a staircase to a basement hallway. Doors along the hall read Storage, but a door at the end was open and Scott heard McCormick talking. He started slowly in that direction.

"He showed up all badass Mr. Hero, but he's fish food now."

Ali said, "I don't believe you."

"Here's his gun. It's a nice one."

"He'll want that back."

McCormick laughed.

"Don't kill him, Scott."

"What?"

McCormick started to turn as Scott bashed him on the side of the head, splitting skin open, the gash bright red. McCormick groaned, staggering a few steps before he fell on the floor. The .45 slid across the floor. Stiletto collected his knife from one of McCormick's pockets and cut the bonds holding Ali to the chair. She rubbed her wrists and went to McCormick. He hovered between staying awake and passing out.

Stiletto turned to the other woman in the room, Tina Avila, who looked at him with wide eyes.

"Your son is safe," he told her.

Ali left McCormick to pick up Scott's gun.

"Where's the FBI?" she asked.

"It's just us, Ali."

"Good." She raised the pistol.

McCormick was easy to kill after all.

STILETTO DROVE the FBI car around to the back parking lot, where Ali and Tina waited for him. He transferred the M-4, ammunition, and flak jackets to another car—a white Cadillac—placing the gear on the back seat as he spoke.

"Take O'Brien's car and drive to FBI headquarters. Tell them you're waiting for O'Brien. They should be able to reach him."

"Where are you going?" Ali asked.

He handed her the keys. "Fairmont's place."

She kissed him on the cheek, and she and Tina climbed into the government car. Stiletto watched them drive away, then eased into the Cadillac and started the motor. He wondered if it was Califano's car. Probably. He found some humor there. He also expected the guards at Fairmont's place to recognize the car. The confusion might provide an advantage.

· · ·

STILETTO PRESSED the pedal to the floor as he started up the final incline to Fairmont's place, the engine letting out a satisfying growl as the rear wheels dug in and propelled the Cad at Fairmont's gate like a raped ape.

The metal gate screeched and scraped against the car. When he heard a klaxon blare from the house and spotlights popped on throughout the property, he knew his arrival had not gone unnoticed.

He continued speeding up the driveway, the house growing in size as he approached.

Stiletto veered sharply left, off the paved driveway and onto the grass, as a Jeep rounded the side of the house and came his way. The Cad's tires kicked up earth as he sped toward the trees clustered along the estate wall. Potshots nicked his car. At the trees, Scott spun the car perpendicular, rolled out, and stayed low for cover as the Jeep closed in. Opening the back passenger door, he grabbed the M-4, slung the shotgun across his back, and filled his pockets with magazines and spare shells. He reached the cover of the trees as the Jeep arrived. Four gunmen jumped out.

Scott fired full-auto, sweeping from left to right. One gunman fell and the Jeep took the rest of the salvo, windows shattering and tires popping. He moved from one spot to another, the ground under him dry, the tree branches not very thick. Return fire cut branches in two and the bits plopped nearby. One gunman lay flat on the grass near the wrecked Jeep, low-crawling Scott's way. Stiletto stitched the shooter with a burst, and he stopped moving.

Stiletto moved left, staying close to the wall where there was enough of a gap between the wall and trees to move. He had to keep his head down to avoid low branches. Return fire behind him came nowhere near.

The brush thickened, and Stiletto stopped. He couldn't just plow through anymore. He dropped flat at the edge of the grass. The two gunners had left the Jeep and were stepping gingerly toward the tree line where he had been previously.

One of the gunners pulled ahead and parted leaves and branches, and Stiletto shot the man behind him. As the man fell, his partner pivoted and tried to make the Jeep, but he collided with the dead gunner and tumbled onto the grass. As he stuck his head up, Stiletto put a bullet through his left eye. The man jerked once, a spray of red hanging briefly in the air as he fell.

Stiletto ran along the tree line where it circled the property, leading closer to the house. The klaxon finally cut off. Somebody else *was* inside, and probably not just Fairmont.

How many more?

Where was the guy with the Doberman?

Scott broke right and ran across a patch of grass to the patio, and somebody fired at him from an upstairs window. He landed hard on the concrete as he rolled, the slung shotgun digging into his back. He hoped the roll hadn't damaged the barrel. He came up on one knee near a glass table, which shattered into a trillion pieces as gunfire struck it. Stiletto ignored the glass that bit into his cheek and blasted the man in the upper window, leaving him hanging half out with a trail of blood and tissue running down the outer wall.

Stiletto's next salvo pierced the patio door, then the M-4 locked open, empty. He slapped in another mag. A dog growled and barked and the Doberman raced out of the house, paws skidding on broken glass as he charged at Scott. Stiletto fired once and the Doberman yelped and tumbled across the patio, coming to a dead stop inches from Scott.

How many more?

Only one way to find out.

He entered the house, using a couch for cover as he scanned the room. Nobody. Fairmont had a taste for expensive furnishings and decorations, judging by the high-end seating and walls adorned with a Rembrandt and a Picasso. Scott moved down a short hallway to another sitting room. More of the same, and still no hostile contact.

As he climbed a winding staircase to the second floor, Stiletto heard a voice from an open doorway at the end of the hall. He advanced in that direction, and the voice continued. A one-sided conversation: a man on a telephone. Stiletto stepped through the doorway.

Max Fairmont stopped talking and yelled into the phone, "Rollins, he's here!"

Stiletto fired once, turning the hand holding the phone into a bloody stump.

Fairmont fell out of his chair, screaming and clutching the stump to his chest as he curled up on the carpet, his white shirt now soaked red. Stiletto didn't even leave the doorway. He took aim and put another round through Fairmont's head. The screaming stopped and Fairmont lay still, blood soaking into the carpet, bits and pieces of him splattered all over.

Scott's ears rang from all the shooting, but his

hearing wasn't so damaged that he didn't notice engine noises from the front of the house.

Stiletto raced down the stairs to the front, where he parted a curtain. Four carloads of armed men exited their vehicles. One of them shouted commands in Farsi. Stiletto didn't need to look too hard at the leader to know his identity.

Shahram Hamin.

One spare mag for the M-4, loose rounds for the shotgun, and his pistol against seventeen hardened Iranian operatives toting AK-47s. Stiletto shook his head. This was going to be a whopper.

He slipped from the window and hustled to the kitchen, where he followed a door out to the garage and another to the side yard. Across the grass was a mother-in-law unit complete with front windows. Hamin would lead his men inside the main house first, spread outside for a search. All he had to do was nail one of them for a chance at an AK and fresh ammo.

Scott left the garage and ran for the unit.

Somebody started shouting and gunfire followed, kicking up dirt around him. He crashed into the door, but the solid wood didn't yield. More gunfire slammed into the small house. Scott twisted the doorknob and rolled inside.

Automatic weapons fire punched through the windows. Scott stayed low and crawled to a bed against the far wall. The shooting intensified, a nonstop volley of hot lead that shredded the walls and punched into the bed. Scott kept his face in the carpet.

Stiletto looked around. No back door, no back windows. He crawled over the debris-strewn carpet to a bathroom, dug out his pen-flash, and shined the light around. No windows there either. The voices outside were getting closer.

Running into the mother-in-law unit now seemed like the dumbest thing he'd ever done.

Stiletto looked at the front windows and watched the enemy approach. Two of them, AKs at the ready.

If this was to be his last stand, he was going down with a gun in his hand.

He ran to the windows and fired the M-4 full-auto. The chests of the two Iranians split open and sprayed bloody mist everywhere. The M-4 ran dry, and Stiletto discarded it. The shotgun next filled his hands. Iranian agents were running for cover. He pumped the action, fired, pumped, and fired again. Two down, one miss. He pumped and fired again. Third enemy down. Return fire zipped through the walls. Stiletto let another blast go and dropped to reload, feeding the Magnum cartridges in one at a time. He moved steadily, as if programmed. His fingers didn't shake, and his heart rate remained normal.

He rose to point the Remington out the window once more. An Iranian only a few steps away tossed a road flare through the window frame. It bounced off the wall behind Scott, the small house filling with an orange glow. Scott blasted the thrower in the belly, and he landed on the grass, wailing in agony.

The flame spread along the back wall to the roof, thick smoke filling the space. Stiletto wiped his eyes, held his breath, and fired two more loads. He didn't even see if he'd scored any hits. He dropped to the carpet again and exhaled, sucking in more air, then coughing and retching.

Hands grabbed him and hauled him across the carpet. Stiletto reached for the shotgun but grabbed only air as the hands dragged him outside.

A blow to the back of his head dropped him flat but he didn't lose consciousness. His vision spun, and his body burned with pain. More hands stripped off the topcoat and snatched his pistol.

More rifle butts hammered into his back and

he yelled, too battered to move. The blows landed again and again.

"We need him alive!" Hamin commanded. "We'll take him back to Tehran."

The beating stopped, and he was lifted by either arm and dragged toward the cars. Sweat stung his eyes and made his blurred vision worse.

The hands let him go, and he fell at somebody's feet. He couldn't lift his head.

"We have plans for you," Hamin said, standing above him.

Another sound broke through his shaky consciousness. It was unmistakable—the whipping rotor blades of a helicopter.

The Iranians scrambled, cars starting, Hamin shouting orders. Scott was lifted once again, only to be abruptly let go. Gunfire filled the air and men screamed.

A voice from the chopper echoed from a loud-speaker.

"This is the FBI. You will drop your weapons and surrender."

Darkness wrapped around Stiletto and he passed out.

. . .

THE FBI CHOPPER HAMMERED ABOVE, the rotor wash blowing like a hard wind. Leaves and yard debris flew everywhere. As his men fired on the chopper and the men in the chopper fired back, Shahram Hamin ran for cover behind one of the cars. His second lieutenant, Harum Mahmoud, landed beside him.

Sirens. Revving engines. More federal cars sped onto the property, the cars stopping on the grass and armed agents pouring out to engage. A spotlight from the chopper lit the property almost like day.

Mahmoud asked, "What do we do?"

Hamin saw the keys in the ignition and gestured for Mahmoud to get in. Mahmoud climbed in back. Hamin took the wheel.

"We go to the wall, and we jump," Hamin said. The engine roared to life, and Hamin floored the accelerator.

"They see us!"

Stray shots thumped into the car. The headlamps picked out the Jeep that Stiletto had fired on earlier and Hamin steered for it. He stopped the car beside the wreck, and the Iranian agents jumped out to help themselves to the dead men's weapons and ammo. Mahmoud fired at pursuing

FBI agents as Hamin pushed through the brush to
the wall. He slung the sub-machine gun over his
back and hauled himself up and over the wall.
Mahmoud followed a second later. They broke into
a run down the slope.

"Now what?" Mahmoud asked.

Hamin pointed out another large house close
by. "They'll have a car."

Hamin saw good fortune as they neared the
street. Gunfire from the Fairmont house and the
echoing voice from the chopper were loud and
clear in the cul-de-sac below, and people were
outside their homes to get a peek at the action.
Some were still dressed, and others wore robes and
slippers.

At the sight of the two armed men, some
screamed and ran back into their homes. Hamin
and Mahmoud ran to the house on the left, where a
man and his wife stood near a black Porsche
Cayenne. The man froze in place as the armed
Iranians rushed across the yard, but the wife
screamed and ran for the front door. Hamin fired a
few feet in front of the woman, concrete chips
pelting her legs, and she stopped long enough for
Hamin to grab her around the neck and rotate to
face the husband.

Mahmoud shoved the snout of his gun in the husband's face.

Their neighbors screamed and yelled for each other to call the police.

Mahmoud demanded, "Keys! Keys to the vehicle, *now*!"

The man remained frozen in place.

"Keys!"

Hamin squeezed the wife's neck. She stiffened against him and let out another yell.

The husband finally broke his trance. He turned toward Hamin, his face twisted in worry.

"Okay, don't hurt her!"

The husband ran inside with Mahmoud on his heels. Hamin held the woman tight. Her neighbors shouted at him, "Let her go! We called the cops!"

One brave soul in a bathrobe that barely hid his bulging stomach marched across the street with a big, shiny handgun. He raised the muzzle at Hamin.

"You better let her go, you fuckin' A-*rab*."

Hamin fired a burst into the air, and suddenly the American Couch Commando wasn't so brave. He ran back across the street, a high-pitched squeal echoing in his wake, bathrobe flapping, and dived into the bushes in his yard.

Mahmoud ran out holding keys.

"Let's go!"

Hamin shoved the wife to the side and joined Mahmoud in the SUV. The Iranians backed out and sped away, the shocked gazes and expressions of the witnesses lingering behind them.

"Where to?"

"Just drive," Hamin ordered. He stowed the sub-machine gun on the floor.

"We have half a tank," Mahmoud reported.

Hamin mumbled OK and dialed Rollins on his cell.

"Where are you?" Rollins asked.

"On the run." He described what had happened at the Fairmont estate.

"Same here."

"We have a problem, though."

"The krytrons, I know. They're still at the warehouse. The Feds haven't moved on it yet. They only found Califano's body a short time ago."

"We need to get there before they do," Hamin said. "What about moving them out of the country?"

"Try Califano's contact first," Rollins said. "If that falls through, I have a few ideas we can try."

"We don't have a lot of time to narrow it down to one that will work if our first option fails."

Hamin ended the call.

"So?" Mahmoud said.

"Back to the safe house," Hamin replied.

"It won't be—"

"Safe for long, yes. We need to ditch this vehicle and get a few things."

Hamin dialed another number.

At the safe house, the Iranian agents grabbed spare clothes and weapons, loading the items into the trunk of a tan Buick parked in the drive. The rush of combat had worn off and they both felt waves of fatigue, but they powered on, driving across town to the Dogpatch neighborhood.

Dogpatch, on the edge of the bay, had once been solely industrial, but in the last twenty years, more and more residential areas had sprung up within the neighborhood. Close to the water, though, it remained solely industrial.

Mahmoud turned the Buick onto 20th Street and drove slowly, passing an auto shop, a flooring manufacturer, a public storage complex, and the warehouse of a welding equipment rental company. Beyond the welding place sat another warehouse that bore no company name or sign of any kind.

Mahmoud parked beside the building and left the engine running.

A cold wind blew off the water, biting through Hamin's light jacket. The blazing lights of the East Bay shoreline shimmered across the bay. The surrounding area, bathed in black, offered no indication of friend or foe. It appeared that Califano's men had run off. Hamin entered the warehouse through a squeaky door.

In the darkness of the interior, Hamin snapped on a flashlight. He spent ten minutes searching through stacks of crates and boxes before he found the locked black case he wanted. He lifted the lid to count the twenty glass-tubed krytrons in their foam packing and brought it back out to the car. There were two other cases, but the Buick was fully loaded. They'd have to accept the loss.

"No guards?" Mahmoud asked.

"Everybody has run off, I guess," Hamin said.

"Where to next?"

"Let's find a motel."

. . .

STILETTO AWOKE IN A HOSPITAL BED, plugged into an IV drip and several monitors. He took a woozy look around the room and saw Toby O'Brien looking out the window. The light blasting through the glass blacked out some of the G-man's features.

"Toby." His voice cracked as he spoke.

O'Brien turned and smiled.

"Welcome back."

"Where..."

"SF General, under tight security. You've been out cold for over twenty-four hours."

O'Brien pulled over a corner chair and sat. "Want to hear how it turned out?"

Stiletto swallowed. His throat felt like sandpaper, so O'Brien went to fill a cup with water from the bathroom sink. He sat down again while Stiletto drank the water.

"Okay," Scott said.

"We got most of them, but Hamin slipped through the net."

"What about Fairmont's buddy Rollins?"

"We're searching for him too."

Stiletto frowned.

"I know, it's not the best update."

"What about Ali?"

"She's safe. Her father's funeral was yesterday. Tina Avila and her son are safe as well."

"And me?"

"You'll live. Sure had a close call, though."

"Don't I know it?"

"And your boss wants you back in Virginia ASAP. He'd like to talk to you about the meaning of the word 'consultant.'"

Stiletto laughed. It hurt, but it also felt good to hurt.

THE NEXT DAY, walking with a cane, patched up and still sore from numerous injuries, Scott Stiletto returned to SFO. Ali Lewis was by his side this time.

They stopped just inside the automatic doors. The line for security seemed to stretch for miles. Cars filled the curbside, passengers dragging luggage into the terminal. They went unnoticed in the stream of activity.

"They couldn't send you a private jet?" she asked.

"Can't have everything."

She hugged him gently. He squeezed back.

"Will you be okay?" he said.

"I'll rebuild. I have a lot of help."

"I'm sorry, Ali."

"You did all you could. More than anyone could ask."

"I'm sorry about other things, too."

"So am I. It wasn't our time. Then. But maybe—"

"What?"

"You can always have a job with me."

"Security?"

"You're an artist, Scott. You could help with clothing design. Do something where people aren't shooting at you for a change."

"I—"

She put a finger to his lips. "Not now."

She kissed him on the cheek. "Good-bye." She turned and walked away.

Stiletto watched her cross the busy street in front of the airport. He kept watching her until she melted into the parking area, out of sight. He stood and watched the place where she had been but wasn't any longer. He wanted to stay. He wanted to follow her. He turned instead and joined the line for security.

As the 747 took off into the cloudy San Francisco sky, Stiletto sat back and closed his eyes. He wondered what Lars Blaser might say. Hamin had escaped. The cycle would continue, unabated.

Others had not escaped. Pito to McCormick to Fairmont, one-two-three. There would be others just like them. There would be others just like Ali. Stiletto was under no illusion that he could stop them all or save them all, but as long as he breathed, Stiletto planned to be the immovable object that the unstoppable force met. Somebody had to be.

CHAPTER THIRTEEN_

A CAR COLLECTED Stiletto at Dulles. The driver, a young woman, said nothing as they sat in traffic on the way back to HQ. A red Corvette, one of the newer models, passed them once traffic opened up, and briefly, Scott wondered if he should rebuild the Trans Am or get something new. Then he dismissed the thought. Why would he *not* want to rebuild?

The driver made it through the CIA entry checkpoint and dropped Scott in front of the building. He moved slowly, every joint aching, but he made it up the steps carrying his suitcase. He proceeded inside.

General Fleming received Stiletto in his office. Scott eased into the chair.

"You're a wreck."

"It's not as bad as it looks, sir."

"Very well. Let's have your report."

Stiletto left nothing out. When he finished, General Ike looked at him for a few moments, tapping a finger on the left arm of his chair. Then he reached for the ever-present glass of water on his desk and swallowed two aspirin. Whatever he had to share was bringing on a migraine. Stiletto didn't know how he managed to function with those things.

"We couldn't have guessed any of this, obviously. The upshot is, Hamin is still on the loose."

"With his krytrons."

"My thoughts exactly."

"He'll need to get them out of the country, and that's how we'll catch him."

"We, not necessarily *you*."

"Sir—"

"You may be improving, but you're in no shape for combat."

"Maybe a little slow."

"'A little slow' may mean the difference between reacting in time to prevent an incident or dying," the general pointed out.

"You have to let me finish this, sir."

General Ike took a breath and went silent again, still tapping the arm of his chair. Stiletto glanced at one of General Ike's paintings, an old wooden Navy ship broken in half and sinking. Sailors were diving into the water or struggling into lifeboats. Scott felt like one of those sailors.

"Who might help Hamin move the krytrons?" the general asked.

"He could call any number of people, but there's one way to find out."

"Your friend Devlin Marcus?"

Devlin Marcus was a smuggler and mercenary captain based in Italy, but also a CIA informant who had proven to be a valuable asset in more ways than one.

"Exactly. This is right up his alley. The Iranians won't risk their own people."

General Ike continued to tap the arm of his chair.

"I'll recall Agent Flynn from the field, and he'll be here in a few hours," the general said. "Call Marcus. I suppose you might as well be there when we catch him."

"I plan to do more than just 'be there,' sir."

. . .

THE SECURE OVERSEAS line rang in Stiletto's ear.

"Yes?"

"It's me."

Stiletto sat at his desk, the straight back of the chair not helping his injuries. He leaned forward on the edge of the chair but that didn't help either, so he stood up and leaned against the wall. That helped a little.

"Ah, my American friend," said Devlin Marcus. "What's today's problem?"

"You might get a call from somebody named Rollins or Hamin..."

"Nothing yet," Marcus said once Scott finished the background. "I'll be sure to drop a dime if I hear something. In exchange for a lot of dimes from you, of course."

"Wouldn't have it any other way," Stiletto agreed. He hung up and sat down again.

He wanted this case finished. He wanted Hamin at the end of his gun. The man had to pay for all that he'd put the Blasers and Ali and Tina Avila and her son through. Hamin had to learn that you couldn't get away with terrorizing others and not face a reckoning. Stiletto intended to be that reckoning.

. . .

When Califano's smuggling contact finally called, Hamin bit off his anger. He couldn't blame Califano's people for lying low, but he and Mahmoud had been switching hotels every day since the raid, constantly looking over their shoulders. It wasn't a happy existence.

"What do you need moved?" the contact asked. His name was Avery.

"Myself, a partner, and a suitcase. Out of the country."

"It'll cost you."

"Money is no object."

"When?"

"Tonight," Hamin told him.

"There'll be a rush charge."

"Fine."

"The first leg of the trip will be by boat," Avery said. "Be at Pier 20 at midnight sharp. Bring fifty thousand in cash."

Hamin checked his watch. Two p.m. Eleven hours to get the money.

"We'll be there," he said.

It wasn't hard to get the money since Hamin had a series of contacts in San Francisco's Iranian community, same as Paris, who either stockpiled funds for such an emergency or pulled cash straight out of cash registers and office safes. A few coded words in the right ears and the goal was met with time to spare.

Hamin stayed plugged in with the local news about the Fairmont raid. The police and FBI had not mentioned his name publicly. They sold the raid as a drug-related arrest, prompting a *Chronicle* columnist to ask why the DEA had not carried out the raid. The Feds kept repeating the story, however.

As Mahmoud drove to the meeting that night, Hamin had to rely on discipline to prevent a side trip to kill the woman, Ali Lewis—a Parthian shot to the American agent who had caused so many problems. But the mission came first. The krytrons had to get to Tehran, despite him having far, far fewer than he'd intended to bring back.

But later on...

Mahmoud stopped in the Pier 20 parking lot. Hamin held the black case and Mahmoud carried a tote bag full of cash as they crossed the lot to the docks where three men waited, one smoking, the other two talking sports. Lampposts cast odd shadows, and water rippled under the wooden planks of the pier. It gave Hamin a general feeling of distrust.

Hamin called, "Hey," as he and Mahmoud neared.

The smoker, Avery, flicked his butt away. He wore dark jeans and a leather jacket over a white t-shirt. The water rippled behind him, and a foghorn blew somewhere on the bay. "Let me see the money," the smuggler said.

Mahmoud opened the tote. The smuggler reached for a stack and ruffled the money. "Looks good. No time to count it, we gotta go."

"Which boat?" Hamin asked.

"Big one down there."

"The one with no lights on? Doesn't look like anybody has prepared it."

"What are you saying?" Avery growled, stepping closer. He partially blocked Hamin's view of the other two men.

Mahmoud's view was not obstructed.

"Gun, Shahram!"

Mahmoud, holding the money in his left hand, dug a pistol from his coat with his right as the smuggler's associates drew their own. Mahmoud fired once, and then again. The associates dropped with dead-center headshots.

Hamin bent and rolled against Avery's midsection, elbowing the smuggler in the solar plexus. Hamin rolled free, holding the black case close to his body. Mahmoud shot the smuggler twice. His body flopped on the planks, blood dripping through the spaces between the boards.

"Let's get outta here!" Hamin said. "Fast!"

They ran back to the Buick and did exactly that.

After they'd driven a few blocks, Hamin pounded on the dash and door panels and let out a scream. Mahmoud remained stoic, but he gripped the steering wheel tightly.

Hamin took a deep breath and took out his cell phone. He called Rollins.

"You better have a plan," Hamin told the go-between. "We are out of options."

"I'm glad you called," Rollins said. "You'll be happy with my answer. How about a drive to Mexico?"

"And then what?"

"A chopper ride, of course."

THE PHONE RANG.

"Yes?" Stiletto said.

"Bingo. Your man Rollins called me," Devlin Marcus said. "The plan is for my guys to pick up Hamin and his lieutenant at an abandoned monastery in Mexico, just over the Arizona border."

"Pick up how?"

"Chopper. I don't have anybody in the US, so this is the next best option. Hamin is heading to the monastery. Rollins is flying to Madrid to transfer funds. He won't do that remotely."

Stiletto hurriedly scribbled the information on a sheet of paper.

"Can you fly a chopper?" Marcus said.

"Yes, but I have another idea."

HAMIN AND MAHMOUD took turns driving south to Los Angeles, stopping for twenty-four hours before continuing to San Diego.

The drive to Arizona along the 8 freeway, was uneventful, and they followed the directions to 95 in Yuma and turned south for the final stretch to the border crossing.

They followed the 95 past Friendship Park to a small border checkpoint. Dogs sniffed the car, and a border agent ran a mirror under the chassis. They had ditched their weapons, and carried only a small amount of cash. The fifty thousand had been returned to the network, and there would be no risk to the infrastructure of his organization. Rollins was footing the bill this time, and there was no need to take a chance by crossing the border with a carload of guns and money.

But Hamin felt naked without a gun.

They passed the inspection with only the usual delay, and Mahmoud drove across the border into Mexico.

MORE LONG HOURS OF DRIVING.

They gassed up just over the border for the ride to the monastery. Hamin tried not to be nervous, but after the incident with Avery, he couldn't sit still. All he had was Rollins' word. He'd feel better when he and Mahmoud were aboard the promised helicopter. At least they were out of the US. That alone was a major victory.

They continued the slow drive along a rutted dirt road, stopping to avoid stray cows and move rocks out of the way.

When they finally reached the empty adobe-walled monastery, even the Buick seemed exhausted. Mahmoud shut off the motor, and the engine started ticking as it cooled.

Hamin looked around. Hills here and there, and tall mountains in the far distance. The heat of the sun wrapped around them like the tentacles of an octopus.

"How long do we wait?" Mahmoud said.

Hamin checked his watch. "We arrived ahead of schedule. Shouldn't be more than an hour or two."

"Let's get out of this heat. I don't think this place is going to be very comfortable, though."

Hamin retrieved the black case from the trunk and followed his lieutenant into the building.

CIA AGENT JIMMY FLYNN flew the chopper eastbound toward Hamin's location. They had collected the Bell Jet Ranger from Marcus's contacts in Guadalupe Victoria. Stiletto rode in the passenger seat in his desert camo fatigues, still sore and grateful for the chopper's air conditioning. The heat of the sun still broke through the Plexiglas and gave the A/C a run for its money.

Flynn dropped low outside city limits and

guided the Bell helicopter over the rises and dips, the desert terrain below flashing by.

Stiletto had a scoped M-1A rifle between his knees. The plan called for him to take a sniping position a mile from the monastery. Flynn would draw Hamin out with the chopper, then lights out. Good night, Hamin.

The dash-mounted GPS flashed an alert that they were one mile out from the monastery. Flynn slowed to a hover, kicking up a large cloud of dust, and Stiletto jumped out. It wasn't the best idea. The jolt of the landing hurt, but Scott ignored the pain as he ran through the dust cloud. Flynn lifted off.

Stiletto ran about fifty yards as the chopper continued on, the whipping blades replaced by quiet. Scott found a small rise and dropped there, setting the M-1A on a two-legged mount and sighting through the scope. The monastery showed up in the eyepiece as if he were standing next to it.

The chopper flew over the monastery once, circling it several times before two heads appeared in a doorway. Flynn continued his orbit until Hamin, holding the black case, and another man ran into the open space outside. Flynn flew in a long circle and started to descend. Hamin waved. Stiletto pulled the trigger. Hamin's number two went down with his head split open by the .308 boat-tail.

Hamin started to run. Stiletto tracked him and fired again, and the shot hit Hamin low in the back. The Iranian agent tumbled into the dirt, the black case flying from his grasp.

Stiletto ignored his own discomfort as he ran to the fallen Iranians. The one with the split head was quite dead, no question. Hamin, unable to move, waited. The .308 had snapped his spine in two. Blood soaked the dirt beneath him.

Stiletto slowed to a stroll as he approached Hamin and stopped beside the fallen man. Hamin could only move his eyes, his breathing hoarse through his open mouth. Stiletto knelt to make eye contact. The chopper's rotor wash blew dust into their faces, but unlike Hamin, Stiletto was able to raise a hand to shield his eyes. He smiled, winked, and stood. He went to the black case, opened it, and one by one, smashed the glass tubes with the butt of the M-1A.

Flynn landed ten yards away. Stiletto hopped aboard and pulled the door shut. He watched Hamin stare at him as Flynn lifted off.

"You left him alive," Flynn remarked. He climbed into the clear blue sky.

"Got him in the spine. If the sun doesn't get him, the buzzards will."

Flynn smiled.

Stiletto plugged in a satellite phone and called headquarters. After a few minutes, he was patched through to the general. He gave his update.

"Excellent," the general said. "Our other team caught up with Rollins in Madrid. He's in custody."

"I'm sure he'll have a lot to share with us."

"It feels good to finally win."

"Indeed, sir. See you shortly." Stiletto ended the call and turned to Flynn. "Let's go home."

Stiletto settled back in the seat as the chopper climbed. It wouldn't be hard to talk the boss into giving him some time off. It might be nice to visit Montana.

A LOOK AT THE GLINKOV
EXTRACTION (SCOTT
STILETTO 3)_

The Glinkov Extraction is the third book in the hard-edged, action thriller series — Scott Stiletto.

AN AUTHORIZED MISSION TO rescue a friend may be the last adventure of Stiletto's career ... or his life.

A coup stirring in Russia to overthrow President Putin faces the wrath of Moscow police and government agents. Suspects are arrested or assassinated. Survivors run for their lives, including Vladimir Glinkov, a friend of Scott Stiletto.

Glinkov desperately calls for help, but the U.S. government will not get involved. Despite his pleas to aid a friend in need, Stiletto is ordered to stand down.

But Stiletto will not do nothing while a friend suffers. He'll get Glinkov and his family out of Russia before they're executed... or die trying.

"...Stiletto is every bit as exciting, gritty, and tough as [Vince] Flynn's Mitch Rapp!..."

COMING SOON FROM BRIAN DRAKE AND WOLFPACK PUBLISHING.

A twenty-five year veteran of radio and television broadcasting, Brian Drake has spent his career in San Francisco where he's filled writing, producing, and reporting duties with stations such as KPIX-TV, KCBS, KQED, among many others. Currently carrying out sports and traffic reporting duties for Bloomberg 960, Brian Drake spends time between reports and carefully guarded morning and evening hours cranking out action/adventure tales. A love of reading when he was younger inspired him to create his own stories, and he sold his first short story, "The Desperate Minutes," to an obscure webzine when he was 25 (more years ago than he cares to remember, so don't ask). Many more short story sales followed before he expanded to novels, entering the self-publishing field in 2010, and quickly building enough of a following to attract the attention of several publishers and other writing professionals. Brian Drake lives in California with his wife and two cats, and when he's not writing he is usually blasting along the back roads in his Corvette with his wife telling him not to drive so fast, but the engine is so loud he usually can't hear her.

You will find him regularly blogging at
www.briandrake88.blogspot.com

Find more great titles by Brian Drake and Wolfpack Publishing, here:
https://wolfpackpublishing.com/brian-drake/

Made in the USA
Las Vegas, NV
07 September 2024

94947491R00135